Her heart stuttered.

She remembered every excruciating moment of the days and nights she'd lain tied in that dark cabin. The burn of the ropes against her wrists. The incredible thirst. The emptiness like a chasm inside her. She couldn't push it out of her mind. She'd been worried about Reed then, too. The helplessness was the worst. It ate into her soul until there was nothing left but bitter darkness. She couldn't sit here in the dark waiting for Reed. Or wait for the killer to find her.

Oh, God, please, don't let this happen again.

Just then, Reed stepped around the corner and rushed to her side, holding her on her feet. Her body dissolved, as if the muscle holding her upright had turned to quivering goo. The way she was shaking she didn't know if her legs would carry her.

Worse, she didn't want to leave the protection of Reed's arms....

ANN VOSS PETERSON

EVIDENCE OF MARRIAGE

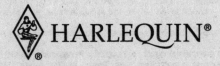

HARLEQUIN®

TORONTO • NEW YORK • LONDON
AMSTERDAM • PARIS • SYDNEY • HAMBURG
STOCKHOLM • ATHENS • TOKYO • MILAN • MADRID
PRAGUE • WARSAW • BUDAPEST • AUCKLAND

To my father, Gil Voss, who is nothing like Dryden Kane.

ISBN-13: 978-0-373-22931-4
ISBN-10:   0-373-22931-3

EVIDENCE OF MARRIAGE

www.eHarlequin.com

Printed in U.S.A.

ABOUT THE AUTHOR

Ever since she was a little girl making her own books out of construction paper, Ann Voss Peterson wanted to write. So when it came time to choose a major at the University of Wisconsin, creative writing was her only choice. Of course, writing wasn't a *practical* choice—one needs to earn a living. So Ann found jobs ranging from proofreading legal transcripts, to working with quarter horses, to washing windows. But no matter how she earned her paycheck, she continued to write the type of stories that captured her heart and imagination—romantic suspense. Ann lives near Madison, Wisconsin, with her husband, her two young sons, her Border collie and her quarter horse mare. Ann loves to hear from readers. E-mail her at ann@annvosspeterson.com or visit her Web site at annvosspeterson.com.

Books by Ann Voss Peterson

CAST OF CHARACTERS

Diana Gale—A victim most of her life, Diana has vowed to stand on her own two feet. Even if that means turning her back on the only man she's ever loved and taking on her father–serial killer Dryden Kane.

Detective Reed McCaskey—Overprotective to a fault, Reed takes his vow to protect and serve seriously. Especially when it concerns Diana Gale. But when she takes on Dryden Kane, even he might not be able to protect the woman he loved and lost.

Dryden Kane—There's a copycat killer loose on the streets, and notorious serial killer Dryden Kane is pulling the strings.

Detective Nikki Valducci—This cop might look like a cover girl, but she's tough as nails. Will she be tough enough to help McCaskey get his man?

Detective Stan Perreth—The disagreeable detective is good at his job. But what are his priorities? Stopping a serial killer? Or stopping Reed McCaskey?

Louis Ingersoll—Diana's neighbor wants only what's best for her. And in his opinion, that would be him.

Meredith Unger—Dryden Kane's attorney will go to great lengths to give her clients the representation they deserve. But does that include breaking the law?

Cordell "Cord" Turner—The ex-convict has a chip on his shoulder as complex as his tattoos. And as Dryden Kane's son, is he also a chip off the old block?

Chapter One

Laundromats made good hunting grounds.

Alone, for now, he sat back to wait, listening to the empty rumble of the drier and the tinny radio tuned to the blues. He liked a little blues on a hunting trip. The music was gritty and real and full of pain. Like the sweetness of a dying scream.

He'd never guessed how invincible killing could make him feel. The godlike power of holding life and death in his hands. It had taken a mentor to teach him. To guide him. Until he'd become brave. Until he'd become strong. Stronger than he'd ever imagined he could be.

But it had been too long since he'd tasted that strength. Eight months of fantasizing. Eight months of lying low, waiting for warm weather, waiting for the police and press to grow bored, waiting for word.

Now he was hungry to feel his power.

The glass door swung open and for a moment

the rush of traffic outside eclipsed the low thunk of the bass guitar. The door closed, and a blonde shouldering a duffel trudged past the vending machines and between rows of whirring washers.

He took a deep breath. The air smelled sweet with detergent and fabric softener. Not as sweet as her hair would smell. Not as sweet as the scent of her blood. He'd never understand why women who would never walk down a dark street alone would brave a night like this to wash their laundry. Clean clothes were damn important to some people. He smiled as she came closer.

He could see she was older than the three he'd done last fall. Delicate crow's-feet touched the outer corners of her eyes. Her mouth held the pinched look of a woman who had to work hard to make ends meet. She was probably in her mid-thirties, maybe close to forty. He didn't like older women. They were smarter, not as easily misled.

She glanced at him with narrowed eyes. As if she could see something in him that bothered her.

For a moment he considered walking out, checking the Laundromat down the street. The last thing he wanted was for her to figure him out and give his description to the police. He couldn't afford to give them a gift they didn't deserve.

She opened one of the small, top loaders and sorted whites into it. Bras. Lacy panties.

She was the one.

He looked at her again, more closely this time. If her hair were a little lighter in color, if her lips were set in a cruel smile, she would look like his mother. He liked that thought. It got his blood pumping. Maybe he could even dress her in the slutty miniskirts his mother used to wear. And one of those oversize shirts with big shoulder pads that had gone out in the eighties.

He shifted in his chair. If he went on fantasizing about what he was going to do, his growing arousal would tip her off for sure. Besides, after eight long months, he'd fantasized long enough. He wanted action.

Humming along with the radio, she pulled a small bottle of detergent from her duffel, measured it into the cap and poured it into the machine.

He stood up and crossed to one of the machines whose wash cycle had finished. Pulling out wet jeans, he threw them in a drier near the woman. He pasted his most innocent and pitiful expression on his face. "Excuse me."

She glanced up at him, offering a stranger's smile, brief and insincere.

"My girlfriend told me to get some of those drier sheets. She says she doesn't like the smell of my clothes. If you don't mind my asking, what kind do you use?"

She dipped a hand into her duffel and pulled out a pink box. "These are the best. They smell the best and do a great job controlling static. Do you want to try one?"

Crossing the aisle, he reached into his pocket. He had to be fast. He couldn't let her catch on. Not until he had her where he wanted her. He tilted his head at the pink box, as if he really gave a damn about fabric softener. "Oh, I've seen commercials for that kind." He reached out as if he intended to take a closer look at the package. Instead, he grabbed her arm.

Her eyes flew wide. She pulled back, trying to free herself, trying to fight.

He whipped his hand out of his pocket and stabbed the syringe into her arm. He held her as she fought. Finally the drug took effect, and she swayed and stumbled into him.

Moving quickly, before anyone else wandered into the Laundromat, he pulled his laundry bag over her head. When he'd pulled it down past her waist, he positioned her swaying body next to a laundry cart and flopped her over. Lifting her by the hips, he heaved her into the cart.

A tinge of pain shot through his back. They were always heavier when they were dead-weight. Once he let her loose in the forest, once she was fighting for her life, he wouldn't have to worry about back strain. Then the pain would all be hers.

He stuffed her feet into the oversize bag, pulled the drawstring closed and tied it. Smiling to himself, he wheeled the cart to the exit and his waiting van outside.

Yes, Laundromats were great for hunting. And he'd just bagged himself some prey.

Chapter Two

Diana Gale had done everything she could think of to make her twin sister's post-wedding gift opening a memory to cherish. She'd decorated her apartment with purple irises and white streamers. She'd poured mimosas and coffee for Sylvie's handful of out-of-town friends. And, not much of a cook herself, she'd made brunch reservations at one of Madison's best restaurants. But as Sylvie sat on the couch next to her groom and tore open the card attached to the last silver-and-white package, Diana knew something was wrong.

Sylvie's face blanched. Clutching at the gift, she looked to her new groom with stricken eyes. "Bryce."

"What is it?"

Sylvie spread the wedding card before Bryce Walker. She looked up at Diana.

She didn't have to say who the gift was from.

Diana knew by the alarm shining in her sister's blue eyes—eyes identical to hers. And *his.*

A tremor crept up Diana's spine, raising the hair on the back of her neck. She hadn't spoken to their birth father in months, neither had Sylvie, but a day hadn't passed that they didn't think about him. Now the door of communication she'd thrown open would never be able to fully close.

"Who is it from?" One of Sylvie's friends who'd traveled up from Chicago for the wedding eyed Sylvie with a curious smile.

Diana plastered a smile to her own lips. Lisa might have been one of Sylvie's workmates from her previous life, but there was something about the woman Diana didn't trust. It was as if she were constantly on the prowl for a wisp of gossip to provide herself with excitement, even at someone else's expense. The last thing either Sylvie or Diana needed was for Lisa and Sylvie's other friends at the morning gift opening to learn who had given this particular gift. "Just someone we know."

Leaning the gift against the side of the couch where she and Bryce sat, Sylvie pushed to her feet. "You'll have to excuse me. I'm not feeling so well." She darted from the room and down the hall toward Diana's bathroom.

Bryce handed the card to Diana and started after his bride.

She gripped the card with trembling hands. Opening it, her eyes flew to the simple message scrawled beneath the wedding verse. A message from their father, serial killer Dryden Kane.

A father should have the privilege of walking his daughter down the aisle. I miss my girls. I look forward to your visit.

A newspaper clipping lay between the tissue folds inside the card. Several months old, the newspaper article was dated October of the previous year.

Copycat Killer Claims Three

Cold filtered through her blood. She knew Dryden Kane's silence wouldn't last forever. She knew he'd find a way to contact them. She also knew in her bones that her hometown of Madison, Wisconsin, hadn't heard the last of the killer who was copying Kane's crimes—a man the police believed was carrying out the orders of Kane himself.

"Is Sylvie okay?" Lisa looked down the hall, eyes glowing with predatory interest.

"Maybe we should see if she needs anything," another friend offered.

"What is in that card?" asked a third.

Waving off their questions, Diana eyed the gift that leaned against the side of the couch still shrouded in its silver-and-white wedding-bell paper. She had to think. She had to figure out what to do. She had to talk to Sylvie and Bryce. But in order to do any of those things, first she must deflect Sylvie's friends and their curiosity.

She made a show of looking at her watch. "Why don't you guys head down to the restaurant?"

"The restaurant? Now?" Lisa shook her head. "I think we should help Sylvie."

"Bryce *is* helping her."

"There's only so much a man can do." Lisa stood up from her chair and plopped her hands on her hips. "I've been friends with Sylvie longer than any of you. It's my duty to help her through this."

Diana tried to tamp down her annoyance. Lisa might have known Sylvie the longest, but she had no clue about what they were dealing with. "Making sure the restaurant doesn't give away our table will be the most help, Lisa. Really."

Lisa frowned. Apparently she wanted more excitement than securing a spot for brunch would provide.

"Lisa, please." Diana offered her best pleading smile, praying the woman had the sense to stop pushing. "It would really help out."

Reluctantly, Lisa nodded. "All right. But if the three of you don't join us soon, I'll be back to check on you." She gathered her posse and headed out of Diana's apartment.

As soon as the door shut behind them, Diana set

the card on the counter and rushed to check on Sylvie. She tapped on the bathroom door.

Bryce stepped out into the hall and closed the door behind him.

"How is she?"

"Sick. I'm sure all of us feel that way to some extent."

Diana couldn't agree more. But Diana's nausea was mixed with a heavy dose of guilt. "Is she going to be okay?"

Bryce paused, studying Diana's face. "We were going to wait to tell people, but you might as well know now."

"Know what?"

"Sylvie's pregnant."

"Oh, Bryce! That's wonderful. I know how much you both want kids. Congratulations."

"Thanks." Bryce smiled despite the concern still cloaking his brow. "But I'm worried about her. Especially with all this."

"You're leaving on your honeymoon tomorrow. She won't have to worry about it. At least not for a few weeks."

"If I can convince her to go."

"She has to go."

He shrugged. "You know Sylvie. She's worried about you."

Diana shook her head. Her sister's concern for

her would be touching, if Diana weren't guilty of bringing this evil into Sylvie's life in the first place. "I'll be fine."

He gave a shallow nod, as if he wasn't so sure.

"Trust me. I can take care of myself this time. You and Sylvie have a baby to think about."

He nodded, but again, his agreement wasn't convincing.

She knew he was remembering last October, when he and Sylvie had saved her from becoming the victim of a grief-stricken man's revenge. But that wasn't all that had happened during that time. There had been more. Far more. "You're thinking of your brother."

"I promised him…I promised myself that I'd find his killer. Kane waving this Copycat Killer in our faces is a little hard to take."

Diana nodded. She knew Bryce believed the man who'd killed three women last fall was also responsible for his brother's death. "Sylvie needs you. And she doesn't need to be worrying about Dryden Kane."

He held up a hand. "I know. Believe me, my priorities are in order."

"What did the doctor say? You know, about her heart condition?" As a child, Sylvie had suffered from heart problems, the reason she had been left behind in the foster-care system while Diana had been adopted. In the year since they'd been reunited, Sylvie hadn't had any health problems, but that didn't mean the extra stress of dealing with Dryden Kane piled on top of her pregnancy wasn't a recipe for disaster.

"He said she should avoid extra stress. And I aim to make sure she takes that advice."

The bathroom door opened and Sylvie stepped out into the hall. Her cheeks looked flushed, her eyes a bit glassy. "If the two of you are done deciding my future, why don't we see what is in that package?"

Bryce cupped her elbow gently in one hand and searched her face. "Are you sure you're up to it?"

She shot him a resigned frown. "I'm pretty sure I'm *not* up to it. But that doesn't mean I'm not going to see what he sent. I'm sure my heart can take that much."

"I didn't mean anything by that." God knew that of the two of them, Sylvie was the strong one. Diana had only to think back to that cabin in the woods for proof.

"I know. You're just watching out for me. What families do, right?" Sylvie offered a smile. "I'm still getting used to that."

"Yeah. What families do." Diana took a deep breath, trying to quell the nervous fear fluttering through her chest and stomach. After all she'd been through in that cabin last fall, she'd sworn she would never be a victim again. She'd be more like her sister. Strong. Independent. And eight months later, she finally felt as if she were making some progress. She'd completed her master's degree and had landed a job teaching English literature that would start in the fall. After a lifetime of depending on others, she'd learned a bit about standing on her own.

She sucked in another breath. If Sylvie was willing to face whatever was in the package, so was she. "Okay. Let's open the thing."

She led Bryce and Sylvie into the living room. Bryce and Sylvie took their places on the couch. Diana propped a hip on the couch's arm. Grabbing the corner of the gift wrap, Sylvie tore a corner of the paper free and slid out a simple black frame holding a family portrait. A father, a mother and two little girls around three years old smiled for the camera. Soft blond hair curled around the girls' nearly identical faces. One of the girls cradled a clown puppet. The other tangled her fingers together in her lap, her face chalky and frail-looking. The mother held her blond head high, her lips pressed into a commanding smile. The father stood behind the three, staring directly into the camera with ice-blue eyes.

The perfect family. The family of serial killer Dryden Kane.

"It's us," whispered Sylvie. "My God, it's us."

Diana stared at the portrait, a mixture of heat and nerves descending into her chest. "I'm so sorry, Sylvie."

"For what?"

"For bringing him into your life." She rubbed her forehead with shaking fingers. "What was I thinking? When I found out he was my father, why couldn't I have just left well enough alone? Why did I have to see him in the first place?"

"Because you needed to know where you came from. You needed to understand who you were."

"Which is what?" The daughter of a serial killer? Her mind shuddered at the thought.

"Which is my sister." Sylvie touched her hand to Diana's arm, her trembling fingers belying the steadiness in her voice. "Sometimes we just need to know. No matter what the consequences. I would have done the same thing, Diana. You know that."

She did. But that didn't make her feel any less responsible. "I have to stop him."

Bryce looked from one sister to the other, worry heavy on his brow. "What are you going to do?"

"I don't know yet. But I know who might." She forced a breath into aching lungs. Although eight months had passed since she'd given him back his ring, the pain pulsing behind her eyes made it feel like yesterday. "I'm going to take the portrait and card to Reed."

Sylvie thrust to her feet. "I'll go with you."

Diana held out a palm as if that would hold Sylvie in place. "You have a baby to worry about."

"I'm pregnant, not crippled."

"No, but you're sick."

She gave a shrug, as if morning sickness were nothing. But the pale sheen to her skin told the real story.

"And you don't want that baby to get sick. Besides, you still have guests to deal with. The last thing we need is to have Lisa storming back, demanding answers."

Sylvie opened her mouth to protest, but Bryce cut her off. "We'll take care of Lisa. Tell Reed to call me."

"Of course."

Sylvie pressed her lips together in a frown. Finally she nodded and gave Diana's arm a squeeze. "We're in this together, Diana. Remember that."

Diana nodded. They *were* in this together. Whether Sylvie deserved to be or not. And now it was Diana's turn to contribute—to bring what she'd started to an end.

"TELL ME THAT'S SYLVIE."

Reed McCaskey glanced up from the reports

scattering the table he and his partner Nikki Valducci had commandeered at the Easy Street Café.

A young woman pushed through the café door and scanned the worn Formica tables and coffee-sipping crowd. From her cascading blond hair and light blue eyes to the soft line of her cheeks that made him ache to protect her, she hadn't changed. And although she and her sister were identical, there was no doubt in his mind which twin he was looking at. He could feel her presence in the churning of his blood. "It's Diana."

His day had started with being kicked out of his office in the City County Building after inmates in the sixth-floor jail had spent the night stuffing whatever they could find down the toilets until sewage had backed up in the first-floor police station. With the station so pungent it had brought tears to his eyes, he'd traded that smell for the burned-coffee-and-stale-grease aroma of the Easy Street Café. At least until the cleanup crew had a chance to do their thing. But as badly as his day had begun, it was about to get worse.

He dropped his gaze to the reports. "Why don't you take this one?"

"Somehow I doubt she's here to see me." Nikki let out a pained sigh. "Aren't you even curious about what she wants?"

"No."

Another sigh.

Of course Nikki wouldn't understand. She always had to stick her nose in everything. Especially things that were none of her business. A good characteristic for a detective—especially one as ambitious as Nikki—but not a trait he appreciated when the subject was him. "Go up to the counter and ask for some refills, will you?"

"Are you kidding? I'm not going to miss this show." Nikki leaned back in her chair and crossed her legs. Picking up her coffee cup, she took a long, leisurely sip.

So much for keeping his pain to himself.

"Reed?"

No matter how braced he thought he was, the sound of Diana's voice hit him in the gut like a full-fledged ulcer. He kept his eyes riveted to the report in front of him. He didn't need a close-up view. He still saw her face nearly every night in his dreams. And in his nightmares. "I'm busy here, Diana."

"Dryden Kane contacted us."

Kane. An extra shot of acid added to his misery. He looked up, searching her face. "When?"

"He sent Sylvie a wedding gift. A family portrait of us as children."

"Nice."

"She's kind of upset."

He could imagine. He knew Sylvie wouldn't

want his pity, but he couldn't help giving it all the same. The poor girl had grown up in foster homes, dreamed of having a family, only to discover her father was notorious serial killer Dryden Kane. To get this "gift" the day after her wedding had to be a blow. "How did the portrait arrive? Delivery service?"

She shook her head. "It didn't come in the mail either. The only thing I can figure is that he must have had someone drop it off at the reception last night." She tensed her shoulders in a protective shiver.

Reed knew what she was thinking. The same thing he was. That someone who'd delivered the package might very well be the Copycat Killer, the serial murderer who had claimed three women's lives the past fall using the same techniques as Dryden Kane. The killer they believed was being controlled by Kane himself. "Do you have the portrait with you?"

Nikki pulled the cup away from her lips. "Fingerprints?"

He nodded.

Diana gestured at the street outside the café. "It's in my car."

"Good. Nikki can take it over to the lab. They can lift the prints there. Maybe the frame will tell us something, too."

"That's not all." She dipped her hand into her

purse and pulled out a large plastic bag with a greeting card inside. She extended it to him.

"A card. I guess he must have read the etiquette books." He opened the card a crack through the plastic-bag cover. Bold handwriting scrawled at the bottom of a wedding verse. *A father should have the privilege of walking his daughter down the aisle. I miss my girls. I look forward to your visit.*

"I'll bet he does," Reed muttered under his breath. The opportunity to emotionally torture his two beautiful adult daughters must be a dream come true for a sadist like Kane.

"There was a newspaper clipping about the Copycat Killer inside, too. It's tucked in the envelope."

Manipulating the bag, he opened the envelope. The slightly yellowed shadow of newsprint peeked from inside. He shook it out into the bag. The headline was more than six months old, originating from around the first time the press had officially named the Copycat Killer. The killer hadn't killed since, at least not that they'd detected. But with summer here, Reed feared the total would start to rise.

The pain in his gut hardened to anger. Diana might not want him to take care of her anymore, but she'd have to accept certain precautions. "You and Sylvie need to move to a hotel for a few days.

I'll arrange for protection." He braced himself for an argument.

Diana merely nodded. "I'm worried about Sylvie. She's pregnant."

Pregnant. So they couldn't wait until the actual wedding to start their family. No surprise. Sylvie and Bryce were so in love and wanted a family so badly, he'd been amazed they'd put off marriage and babies for as long as they had.

The familiar ache bored into his stomach wall. Last October he would have bet the couple married and expecting would be him and Diana. How things had changed. "Aren't they planning a honeymoon?"

"She won't go. She says she doesn't want to leave me alone with this."

"And Bryce?"

"He wants to get his hands on the man who killed his brother, naturally. But he intends to do what's best for Sylvie and the baby."

"I'll see what I can do to convince her. And I'll have an officer assigned to you." He handed the plastic bag to Nikki. "Have the lab check for prints ASAP, then I want it back. The portrait, too."

Nikki set her coffee cup on the table and stood.

He glanced up at Diana, meeting her eyes for as long as he dared. "Is that all?"

"All Kane sent? Yes."

"Then Nikki will go with you to get the portrait."

Diana hesitated, watching him for a moment. "I need to talk to you."

"Nikki can handle it." He nodded to his partner, praying she'd help him out this time. He was at the end of his tolerance. He couldn't stand looking at Diana one more second and pretend she didn't mean anything to him, that he was just doing his job, working on a case like any other. "Go ahead."

A knowing smile playing at the corner of her lips, Nikki made for the café door, her long, dark ponytail swinging down the middle of her back. "Save my seat."

Diana paused a second longer before following. When she finally disappeared through the glass door, Reed lowered his head into his hands.

Even as an awkward teen with more pimples than confidence, he'd never found being near a woman this difficult. But then, it wasn't every day he had to face the woman he'd loved for five years, the woman he'd finally convinced to say "I do," the woman who'd turned around and kicked his guts out.

Minutes passed as he delved into his stack of reports. He'd just reached the bottom of the first pile when the bell on the café door jingled, and the ache returned in full force. And as much as he wanted to blame it on the battery-acid coffee, he knew without looking up Diana was once again heading for his table.

"We need to talk."

"Didn't Nikki take care of things for you?"

"I didn't come here just to hand over the portrait and card."

Of course she didn't. She couldn't let him off that easily, after all. "Why *did* you come?"

"I want to help."

"Help?"

She pulled out a chair and slid into it, plunking her elbows on the table. "I want to go to the prison. I want to talk to Dryden Kane."

"And who is *that* going to help?"

She tilted her head and looked at him as if he were an idiot. "In the card, he wrote that he wants to see us, talk to us, then he put in a news clipping about the killer."

"So you think he wants to talk to you about the Copycat Killer?"

"Don't you?"

"No."

"Then why send the clipping?"

"You haven't seen him for months. Maybe he thought you could use a little incentive. Or maybe…" An extra shot of acid added to the swirl of pain in his gut.

"Maybe what?"

"Maybe it's a threat."

He expected a reaction. She didn't give him one.

And he knew why. "Of course, you've already thought of that, haven't you? That's why you didn't object when I offered police protection."

She averted her gaze, studying a crack in the Formica. "He sent the card to Sylvie. He wrote that bit about her wedding. I'm afraid for her."

"You should be afraid for yourself, too."

"I brought him into Sylvie's life and my own. I have to deal with him."

"By running to visit him? How do you think giving him exactly what he wants is dealing with him?"

"If I can get him to talk to me, to tell me something, anything about the Copycat Killer, maybe you can use it to find him before he kills more women."

"And Kane?"

"If you can get evidence tying him to the copycat, maybe you could justify sending him back into solitary confinement, no matter what kind of lawsuit he won against the department of corrections."

Not a bad idea, except for the part about *her* talking to Kane. "I'm sorry, Diana. It's out of the question."

She leaned forward, her breasts brushing the tabletop. "I know he refuses to talk to anyone. But he'll talk to me."

"I'm sure he will."

"What's the problem then?"

If she really didn't think asking *him* to agree to put her in danger was a problem, he sure as hell wasn't going to point it out. The last thing he needed was for her to cram his need to protect her back down his throat. It was a battle he couldn't win. "My lieutenant will never go for the idea."

"I'll talk to him."

"He's up to his neck in sewage today. I don't think he'll have time for a meeting."

She narrowed her eyes, as if seeing straight through him. "This isn't personal, Reed. I came to you because you're the lead detective on the copycat case."

"Okay. It's not personal. Then don't take it personally when I tell you there's no way in hell you're getting near that prison."

"You can't stop me. I'll talk to Kane on my own. I did it before."

Her words pierced his chest like a well-aimed ice pick. She'd kept a lot of things from him in the months before their wedding—the fact that Kane was her biological father, her visits to the prison, her doubts concerning their marriage. She hadn't trusted him with any of it. "And if I'd known, I would have stopped you then."

"Exactly why I didn't tell you." She pushed back her chair, the metal legs screeching against worn linoleum. "Obviously talking to you about this was a waste of time. I'll just go straight to your lieutenant and see what he has to say." Thrusting herself out of her chair, she turned and marched for the door.

Watching the sharp kick of her hips, Reed gritted his teeth. He knew what the lieutenant would say. Months of no new leads and the return of summer squeezing down on his head, he'd probably jump at her offer. And in light of Reed's past relationship with Diana, it was doubtful the lieutenant would assign him to accompany her to the prison. A more likely choice would be Nikki. Or, heaven help him, the publicity-seeking Stan Perreth. "Wait."

Diana stopped and spun to face him, hair flung over her shoulder, resolve glinting in her eyes, passion flushing her cheeks.

For a second, he couldn't breathe normally.

He must be crazy for considering this. Certifiable. She'd told him she didn't want his protection, hadn't she? Hell, even back when she'd allowed him to take care of her, he'd failed. But somehow none of that, not even the ache of his own battered heart, could make a difference. He might not *want* to accompany Diana into that prison, but he couldn't *live* with the idea of her walking in there alone. Whether he could protect her this time or not, he didn't know. But he was certain to the marrow of his bones that he couldn't stand by and not try. "Give me a second to clean up this mess, and I'll drive you to Banesbridge."

Chapter Three

Diana didn't have to wonder how worried Reed was about her visit with Dryden Kane. He spent the entire hour-long drive to the prison lecturing her about the psyche of the serial killer. The security screening and trek down the halls of the main building he filled with warnings about prison security. By the time they'd reached the tiny observation room next to the room where she would meet her father and he started jotting down a list of approved questions, she'd had enough. "Listen, I'm the one asking the questions. I'm the one who will decide what they are."

Reed paced across the closet-sized space. He stopped and peered at the television monitor showing four chairs arranged around a small table in the adjacent room. The table and one of the chairs were riveted to the floor. "Dryden Kane is a very smart and dangerous man. You may be his daughter, but that doesn't mean he's not going to try to manipulate you just like he does everyone else. In fact, it's probably even more important to him to control you."

"From where I'm standing, you're the one who's trying to control me." She was sorry as soon as the words left her lips. Comparing Reed to Kane wasn't even on the remote edges of fair. Reed was only doing his job. And despite their past together, she had to focus on what she needed to do, too. It was just that no matter how things had changed from the days when she'd been helpless and Reed had been her protector, the fact that she still felt that vulnerable flutter run through her every time he looked at her made her want to do anything she could to push him away. "I'm sorry. I didn't mean that. But I can take care of myself, Reed. I have to take care of myself." She'd learned that the hard way.

"So you've said."

He didn't get it. Maybe he never would. But it didn't matter. She knew how much being dependent on other people had cost her. She had only to close her eyes and she was tied up in that cabin in the woods, waiting for her own death, reaching deep for the strength to see her nightmare through and coming up empty.

She knew Reed would never believe it, but

breaking off their engagement had shattered her heart, too. She hadn't had much of a choice. All she'd been through in that dark forest had taught her she couldn't rely on someone else to take care of her. She had to grow up and do it herself. Even now, seeing the concern in his eyes, hearing the solid logic in his voice, smelling the familiar scent of his skin—a scent that used to make her feel safe—made her want to curl in his arms and forget the whole thing. If she'd stayed with him, if she'd married him, it would have been only a matter of time before she'd have slipped right back into need and dependence.

She'd have been lost for good.

The door on the far end of the interview room swung wide, and two guards led Dryden Kane inside.

She hadn't seen him for nine months, but he hadn't changed. He still looked much younger than his forty-eight years. Young, and fresh and strangely wholesome. But the aura surrounding him was anything but. The air crackled with an oppressive and dangerous energy that crawled up her spine and trembled in her chest. And Diana knew if she dared meet his ice-blue eyes, she'd stare straight into the flat chill of death.

The guards led him to the chair that was riveted to the floor and handcuffed him to its arms. Once Kane was secured, a guard with broad shoulders and kind brown eyes peered up at the camera. "He's ready for you."

Diana took a step toward the door, her knees trembling so hard they teetered on the edge of collapse.

Reed touched her arm. "Don't agree to anything he asks. Don't promise anything. And don't tell him anything personal that he can use against you. At least no more than he already knows."

"I won't."

"And be careful."

Her throat pinched. So much of her wanted to huddle in Reed's arms and never venture out again that the desire sucked at her. "Maybe this was a mistake."

"You don't have to go in there. We can turn around, leave right now."

"Not that. I mean coming here with you."

Reed's lips pressed into a bloodless line. He let his hand fall from her arm.

She knew she should explain the weakness she felt around him, the dependence, the need. But she also knew he wouldn't understand. She'd meant it when she'd told him their involvement wasn't personal. It couldn't be. And it scared her that the urge to make it so seemed to be coming from her even more than from him.

She forced herself to turn away from Reed and focus on Dryden Kane. She couldn't afford to sabotage herself. Not when she needed every bit of strength to take on the man who was her father. "I'll be fine." Taking a deep breath, she pushed the door open and strode into the interview room.

A smile curved Kane's thin lips. "Diana. I'm glad you're here. It's been too long."

She concentrated on stepping to the chair and lowering herself safely into it before she met his eyes. "I need some answers." Her voice sounded remarkably steady, much steadier than she felt.

Kane's smile remained intact. "Are these answers for you or for the police?"

"The police?"

"They are monitoring our conversation, aren't they? Recording it as well?" He nodded toward the small camera positioned high in the corner of the boxlike room.

She couldn't lie to him. He'd never believe her, and she would destroy her credibility with him if she were anything less than candid. If she wanted to get truthful answers, she'd have to give some. "Yes, the police are monitoring us."

"So what answers are the boys and girls in blue after?"

"They want the identity of the Copycat Killer."

"Of course. They've had a snitch in the cell next to me for nearly a year. Hoping I'll talk in my sleep. Why they think I have anything to tell them,

I'll never understand." He shook his head, the fluorescent lights overhead glinting off silver strands running through brown hair. "And what do *you* want, Diana? Why are *you* here?"

"I want to know why you sent that news clipping with Sylvie's gift. Was it a threat?"

"Why would I threaten my own daughter?"

"Then why did you send it?"

"It convinced you to come visit me, didn't it?"

So Reed was right. Kane had included the clipping to manipulate them. He'd controlled the whole situation. Not that it mattered. Even if she'd known his intentions for certain, she wouldn't have changed her response. She'd be here just the same. And she wouldn't believe for a second that Kane didn't intend at least a hint of threat. "Now that you've gotten my attention, what do you want?"

"I want you to tell me about Sylvie's wedding."

She couldn't have heard him right, could she? "Sylvie's wedding?"

"Of course. A daughter's wedding is special to a father. I should have been there. I should have walked her down the aisle." He lifted his hands, jangling his shackles against the chair arms as if to illustrate why he'd failed to make it.

Her mind balked at the image of Kane as father of the bride. She couldn't imagine it. She didn't want to. "You can't be serious."

"Of course I'm serious. That's the worst part about being in here. Missing the important moments in my daughters' lives." He heaved a sigh full of regret. "Though I can't say I'm sorry you rethought your plans to marry that cop."

She resisted the urge to shift in her chair and glance at the camera. Kane had made his displeasure about her intended marriage clear the last time she'd seen him—about a month before her wedding. The wedding that had never taken place.

"He wasn't good enough for you. Cops think they're so smart. They aren't smart. They're nothing."

The deficiencies of cops. One of Kane's favorite topics. And the perfect segue to a less personal thread of conversation. "The cops seem to think you're controlling this Copycat Killer."

His thin lips stretched into a smile, exposing his straight, white teeth. "So maybe they aren't totally stupid."

"Are you admitting you're controlling the Copycat Killer?"

"You know I wouldn't admit that, even if it *was* true. My lawyer wouldn't be happy with me."

His lawyer. The last lawyer who represented him was Bryce. That is, until Kane became unsatisfied with him. Days later, Bryce's brother was murdered. "You have a new lawyer?"

"A man like me always needs a lawyer. And this one offers a few extras besides legal representation."

"Extras?"

"Nothing you have to concern yourself with."

Maybe not, but she was sure Reed would want to look into just what extras his new lawyer might be offering. "So what do you know about this copycat?"

"Why would I know anything?"

Now it was her turn to play him. She summoned what courage she could muster. "False modesty? I never would have pegged you for it."

His smile widened.

"So what do you know?"

"I know he aspires to be me."

"Why?"

"Why not?" He lowered one lid in a wink.

Even after learning Kane was her biological father, even after several visits with him, she still felt a powerful shiver of revulsion whenever he gave her that knowing wink. Coming from him it seemed profane.

She drew in a deep breath. She couldn't let him know he had the power to throw her. Not unless she wanted to lose control of the exchange entirely. "Why is he patterning his kills after murders you committed years ago?"

"He wants the power."

"What power?"

"The power of life and death. It transformed me. It is transforming him." He spoke evenly, matter-of-factly, the way one of her former English literature professors would discuss the intricacies of *Beowulf.*

But despite his tone, his words clamped down her lungs, making it difficult to breathe. "Why copy anyone? Why not do his own thing?"

"Because he doesn't want to be himself."

"He wants to be you." She suppressed a shudder.

He tipped his head in a single nod. "He wants to be transformed."

"And you are helping transform him?"

He chuckled low in his throat. "I've never even talked to him. Never seen him face-to-face. But I must admit, I can't help thinking of him as something of a son." He smiled and glanced at the camera. "Is that enough to satisfy you, Detective?"

Diana could picture Reed's scowl. Clearly there was no way to know if what Kane said had any significance, or if he was just toying with the police.

"Enough of that. I don't want to waste any more of our time together with police business." Kane looked around the stark room. "This place…it weighs on a man's soul. I need to see my daughters. To know you're all right. I want you to visit more. You and Sylvie."

She folded her arms across her chest. Reed's

warning buzzed in the back of her mind. *Don't agree to anything. Don't promise anything.* "I'm afraid that's impossible."

"Impossible? For a man to see his daughters? Why?" His eyebrows dipped low. He actually seemed confused by the suggestion. Hurt.

He had to be playing her.

"Bryce Walker doesn't want me seeing Sylvie, is that it?"

"Bryce has nothing to do with this."

"He really was a lousy attorney." He glanced around the room. "I mean look at this place. The main building is under construction. The cell blocks are old as dirt. A decent attorney could have gotten me transferred to a decent facility, don't you think?"

She didn't answer.

"I'd just hate to think he would try to come between a man and his daughter. Sylvie didn't send me an invitation to her wedding, she didn't come with you to see me." He shook his head. "A girl shouldn't turn her back on her family just because she's married."

Fear for her sister spun through Diana's mind, making her dizzy. She forced herself to breathe. "Sylvie isn't turning her back. She isn't doing anything against you at all. She's just trying to move on with her life."

He studied her, his emotionless eyes boring into

her, through her. "On the day you get married, I want to see you in your wedding dress. Sylvie denied me that privilege, but you won't."

"I'm not getting married."

"You might change your mind once you find someone worthy."

"I've worked too hard to control my own life. I'm not giving it up for a white satin dress." She wasn't giving it up for the opportunity to visit her serial-killer father in prison either. She pushed up from her chair. "It's time for me to go."

"Are you going to cut me out of your life as well?"

She had to remain firm. She couldn't let him push her around. "I have to get on with my life, too."

"You need your father, Diana."

"Goodbye."

"If someone like that professor ever threatens you again, I want to know about it."

She paused, memories of Professor Bertram holding her hostage for days, stripping her and hunting her in the forest swept through her mind. "Why? What would you do?"

"What any good father would do. I would protect you."

"From prison?"

He lifted one shoulder in a shrug. "I'd find a way."

What was he going to do? Sic the Copycat Killer on anyone who crossed her path? Was he forgetting *he* was the reason Professor Bertram had kidnapped her in the first place? That the man was desperate to avenge Kane's brutal murder of his daughter? "I can protect myself." Taking a deep breath, she turned away from Kane and took a step toward the door.

"He has another one, you know."

The tremble in her legs spread through her body, centering just under her rib cage. She turned back to face him. "What did you say?"

"He took her last night. After stopping in at your sister's wedding reception to pay his respects."

"The Copycat Killer?"

"Of course."

"How do you know this?"

"I know a lot of things, Diana. Like the desperation a parent feels when kept away from a child. Especially when she needs you most. I could tell you all about it if you would visit me."

"Where did he take her?"

"I'm not asking you to do anything a good daughter wouldn't do anyway."

She didn't have to close her eyes to see the nightmare she'd gone through in the professor's cabin play out in front of her like a movie. But where the professor was a grief-crazed father after revenge, the Copycat killed for pleasure. And part of his pleasure revolved around torture and humiliation. "You can't let him kill another woman."

"Can't I? What am I going to do about it? I'm in prison."

Her stomach swirled, with anger, with nausea. As much as she wanted to walk away, as much as she needed to retain control over her life, she couldn't let an innocent woman suffer. She couldn't let an innocent woman die. Not if she had a chance to save her. "What do you want me to do?"

"Visit. Like a good daughter." Thin lips pulled back in an icy smile. "I'll see you again tomorrow. We'll have a nice chat."

Chapter Four

"I told you not to promise him anything." Reed paused behind their prison escort's broad shoulders to let the barred door slide open in front of them. He couldn't wait to get Diana out of this damn prison and as far away from Dryden Kane as possible. He knew allowing her to talk to Kane was a bad idea. He'd been right and then some. Now it was all he could do to keep himself from throwing her over his shoulder and hauling her off somewhere the killer would never find her. Door fully open, the three of them stepped up to the next barred door.

Diana shot Reed a frown. "You heard Kane. The Copycat Killer has kidnapped another woman. What would you have me do? Turn my back and let her die?"

The door slid closed behind them, enclosing them in a sally port between two sets of iron bars.

Trapped. Exactly how Reed was feeling right now. Trapped by Kane's manipulations. "You're assuming the copycat actually *has* another woman."

Diana's eyes flew wide. "You think Kane lied?"

"I didn't say that. But I think he *would* say anything it took to convince you to visit."

"You must be able to find out, though, right? I mean, can't you check missing-person reports or something?"

"Nikki's already on it. *If* this woman exists, *if* she's been identified as missing, we'll find her." The door slid open in front of them, allowing them to continue down the long hall to the prison entrance.

"I want to help."

She couldn't be serious. "Like you helped with Kane?"

"What do you mean? I *did* help with Kane. Weren't you paying attention?"

"Enough to hear you promise to visit him *every day.*"

"I didn't have a choice."

"You had a choice, and you made it."

She pushed a stream of air through tight lips. "Didn't you hear anything else he said?"

"I heard it all." He tapped his jacket pocket, his fingertips rapping against the videotape from the camera in the interview room.

"Did you notice what he said about his lawyer? And the copycat? Did you hear him say he thought of him as a son?"

"I heard." And his mind was already whirring wildly, trying to figure out what it all meant. Or if Kane's slips were merely leading them down another path Kane wanted them to take.

"What are you going to do?"

As if he was going to share those thoughts with her. Or worse yet, include her in the investigation. He might not be able to keep her away from Kane, but he could insulate her from the rest. "I'm going to look into it."

"I can help."

They reached another set of bars blocking their way. The broad-shouldered guard, Corrections Officer Seides, punched a button on the wall and all three of them faced the camera, waiting to be buzzed through.

Reed glanced at Diana out of the corner of his eye. "Sylvie and Bryce checked into a hotel. They booked you an adjoining room."

"I'm not going to sit around in a hotel room."

"Yes, you are."

"This is my fault, Reed. If I hadn't had to find out who my birth parents were, if I hadn't visited him in the first place, none of this would be happening."

"You're more powerful than I ever guessed."

He let the sarcasm slide thickly off his tongue. "Kane would have found his copycat no matter what you did."

"Sylvie wouldn't be in danger."

"So that's what this is about. Guilt?" Something he knew far too much about. "So now you're set on sacrificing yourself? You feel you need to visit Kane daily to pay for your sins?"

"Don't psychoanalyze me. I feel like I might be able to help. That's all."

"Congratulations. You helped. Now you're going to stay safe."

"This isn't personal, Reed."

"No, it's not. In this case, it's my job."

"Your job is to serve and protect the citizens of Madison. Not just me, *all* of the citizens."

Her words stung far more than he wanted to acknowledge. He'd given up everything to join the force, devoted everything he had to the job. Being a cop was more than what he did. Being a cop was who he was.

And no one knew that better than Diana.

"What do you want? To spend the day hanging out in a police station that smells like sewage, fetching coffee? Because if you insist on helping, that's all I can offer."

"Sounds like heaven."

"Right."

"I can't think of a safer place for me to be than a police station, can you?"

He blew an impatient breath through his nose. He couldn't argue there. And judging from her victorious smile, she knew it. "If that's what you want…"

"That's what I want."

He waited for the last barred door to slide open. But when he and Diana stepped through it, instead of feeling relief for getting her away from Kane, he couldn't shake the sense that he was only leading her deeper. And that there wasn't a damn thing he could do about it.

REED HADN'T BEEN KIDDING about the smell.

Breathing shallowly through her mouth in an attempt to combat the stench of sewer, Diana wound through misplaced desks and ripped-out ceiling tiles, a foam cup of coffee in each hand. Reed also hadn't been kidding when he'd said he wasn't going to let her play the role of cop. Two hours had ticked by since they'd reached the station, and the biggest thing he'd allowed her to do was make a pot of coffee. At this point, she was so frustrated, she actually needed the caffeine to *calm* her nerves.

She set a cup in front of Nikki and raised the other to her lips. Since Reed had been so open and sharing with her, she'd decided to return the favor. Let him get his own coffee.

Sipping her hot brew, she craned her neck, trying to get a look at Nikki's computer screen. Late-afternoon sun slanted through the high windows in the partially underground first-floor station and glinted off the screen, hiding whatever Nikki was looking at in a blur of glaring light.

Just her luck. "Can I do something to help, Nikki?"

Nikki twisted to glance at her, her lips pressed into an apologetic expression. "Thanks for the coffee."

"No problem." Diana didn't have to look in Reed's direction to feel his glower. Reed's partner hadn't said much, but Diana didn't have to be a mind reader to sense Nikki's sentiments lay on her side. And that Reed wasn't happy about it. She kept her eyes on Nikki. "Have you talked to Kane's lawyer yet?"

"Can't locate her. She's probably out sailing on one of the lakes or whatever it is lawyers do on a Sunday around here."

"Who is she?"

"Meredith Unger," Reed supplied.

Nikki nodded. "She did some criminal work just out of college. But she's stuck to corporate work since. I guess she's branching out again with Kane."

Diana thought back to what Kane had said about her. "What is the 'extra' that Kane referred to?"

Nikki shrugged. "Don't know. She's attractive, in a she-wolf sort of way. It could be that."

Possible, she supposed. But that wasn't what she'd thought of when Kane had mentioned his lawyer in the prison. "Do you think he's manipulating her? Getting her to convey messages between him and the copycat or something?"

"I think we can assume he's manipulating her in some way," Nikki continued. "Kane would probably lose interest in her if he wasn't. The rest, we don't know. Not yet, anyway."

"Why would she take Dryden Kane on as a client in the first place?"

Reed grunted. "The reason all of them take someone like Kane on. Notoriety. They like to see their names in the paper."

"And some women think danger is sexy," Nikki added.

Diana knew that was true, yet she would never understand it. All she'd ever wanted in a man was safety, tenderness, someone she could depend on. Of course, becoming too dependent turned out to be dangerous, too.

She yanked her thoughts from that painful path and focused on the missing-person reports piled on Nikki's desk. "What are you looking for? Missing college-age women with blond hair? Like the women the copycat killed last fall?"

"We'll tell you if we find something, Diana."

Nikki gave Reed a guilty glance, then nodded anyway. "Usually when a serial killer kills several women who look alike, like this killer has done, it indicates the woman's look is part of what turns him on, part of his reason for committing the crime."

When Diana had discovered Dryden Kane was her biological father, she'd read everything she could find on serial killers. And she'd discovered far more than she'd ever thought she wanted to know. "You're thinking the victim's hair color and age are part of his signature."

"Exactly. Age and hair color were the things all three victims had in common. Although we don't know much more than that about the third victim."

The third victim. The woman whose body had been burned and mutilated so badly, police had never been able to determine her identity. For a couple of days, they'd even believed the body to be Diana's.

She pushed that morbid thought from her mind. "I guess my question is, whose signature are we talking about?"

Nikki tilted her head. "What are you thinking?"

Reed cleared his throat, as if warning Nikki not to go too far in including Diana.

Nikki didn't seem fazed.

Diana pushed on. "When Kane was working

up to killing my mother..." Diana swallowed.
Even after all these months, she hadn't gotten used
to the idea that her father had killed her mother.
Somehow that fact was more difficult to process
than her father being a serial killer. She could only
speculate about what that said about her.

Nikki gave her an encouraging nod. "When he
was working up to killing your mother, he looked
for young, blond victims."

"Yes. So when the copycat killed these women,
was he just trying to emulate Kane's signature or
is that part of his own?" Diana looked up at Reed
to gauge his reaction.

Picking up his phone, he punched in a number
and held it to his ear. He walked into a nearby conference room and closed the door behind him.

Diana's cheeks heated. She didn't have to ask
what he thought of her observation. But as much as
his dismissal stung, it was nothing compared to the
realization that, even after all these months, looking
to Reed for approval was as automatic as breathing.

Nikki leaned toward her. "Don't let him bug
you. I think it's a good question. *And* I think it's a
great idea to have you help in this case."

"You do?"

"You bet. The FBI is using more and more pro-
active techniques when it comes to finding un-
identified subjects. I'd say you interrogating your

father has to be on the cutting edge." Admiration filled her voice.

"You really want to get this guy, don't you?"

Nikki smiled. "You have to ask?"

No, she didn't. From the first time she'd met Nikki, she'd felt the hunger under that fashion-model facade. Nikki might look the part of a beautiful bimbo, but she had goals and grit. And heaven help the serial killer who got in her way. "I'm glad you're on this case."

"What do we have here? A mutual-admiration society?"

Diana glanced up at the sound of the deep, cigarette-roughened voice. "Detective Perreth."

"Nice to see you, Miz Gale." Though the growl in his voice sounded anything but pleased to see her, Reed's old nemesis had the nerve to grin, his jowly face taking on the look of a panting bulldog. "Where's McCaskey?"

"Right here." Reed emerged from the conference room. "What do you want, Perreth? Come to enjoy the smell?"

"I've been assigned to the task force."

"Great."

Reed didn't show any reaction, but Diana could guess how he felt about the news.

And how much Perreth was enjoying it. "It might be good if we coordinate what we're going to tell the press. Starting with what Dryden Kane's daughter is doing with her nose in the copycat case."

"We're not going to tell the press anything."

"And you don't think word about who she is will get out now that the copycat is active again?"

Reed stepped close to Perreth, his taller frame towering over the squatty detective. "In the conference room. We need to talk."

The men filed into the conference room and shut the door behind them.

Diana clenched her teeth until her jaw ached.

Nikki laid a hand on her arm. "He's Reed's problem. Not yours."

Nikki was right. Whatever bad feelings Perreth had toward her had come from his conflicts with Reed. She hardly even knew the man. Nor did she want to. His condescending attitude and the cold way he stared at her shouldn't bother her. Of course, they did anyway.

She let out a pent-up breath and turned away from the conference-room door.

Nikki gave her an approving nod. She picked up a stack of missing-person reports from her desk and plunked them in front of Diana. "I could use your help now that Reed is busy dealing with Stan."

Diana took the reports, not bothering to hide the smile on her face. As it turned out, that closed door worked both ways. "Thanks."

"Don't mention it. Three women went missing this weekend. None of them match the copycat's previous victims."

"Three women? In one weekend?"

Nikki waved away her surprise. "They all went missing last night. Chances are they are shacked up with boyfriends or forgot to tell their roommate or husband where they were going. Most show up."

"But some don't."

"Some don't."

Diana shuddered. Just last fall, she'd been missing, just like these women. If Sylvie and Bryce hadn't kept pushing to find her, she would have been one of the ones who never showed up.

She slumped in her chair and focused on the reports. Skimming hair-color and eye-color check boxes for each of the women, she could see what Nikki meant. They didn't match. Two of the women fell into the same college-age group as the copycat's victims, yet one had black hair and brown eyes; the other was a redhead. The third woman was blond, but she was approaching forty.

Diana moved her gaze down the page. Skimming blood type, vehicle information and descriptions of clothes and jewelry, she landed on the section entitled Other Information. Sure enough, a roommate had reported one of the college girls missing, a husband the other. She paged to the last report detailing the older blond woman. The complainant in that case was the woman's mother.

Diana read farther on the blonde's report. Reaching the officer's notes, her eyes landed on the few sentences detailing the circumstances of the woman's disappearance. "Beck's Laundromat. That's only a couple blocks from the restaurant where Sylvie had her reception."

Nikki greeted her comment with raised brows.

"Kane said the copycat abducted a woman right after he dropped off Sylvie's wedding gift." She grabbed the videotape from Reed's desk and stuffed it into the ancient VHS player.

The door to the conference room opened. Without looking, Diana could feel Reed's black eyes boring into her. He didn't say a word, as if he'd heard her comments, as if he already knew what she thought she'd found.

"He told me that right before I left. I'm sure it's here." She pressed Fast Forward and the images of Kane and her twitched double time on the screen. The way she'd felt while talking to him washed over her in a wave. The oppressive fear. The revulsion. The sense that whatever she did or thought, she was merely a puppet in his hands.

Even with the sound muted, their conversation lapped against her mind. "He said something else, too."

"What?" Reed stepped toward her and took the remote from her hand.

She let him have it, concentrating on the memories tightening her throat and rasping along her nerves. "Something about the desperation a parent feels when they've lost a child."

"He was referring to Vincent Bertram kidnapping you."

"I know. But the way he said it was weird. Pointed. What if he meant this woman, too?"

"Possible. If the copycat stalked the victim ahead of time."

She glanced at the missing-person's report lying on the desk. Or the copycat knew what the report said. An uneasy feeling pinched the back of Diana's neck. She shook her head, trying to dispel the feeling and the thought that inspired it. She could feel Perreth watching her from the mouth of the conference room. She knew he beat his wife. Reed's confronting him about it was the cause of the bad blood between them. But any other suspicions she had were pure imagination. "I don't know. Maybe I'm reaching on that. But the location of the Laundromat is still reason to look into this further."

Reed pointed the remote at the player. The images of her and Kane slowed to a natural cadence. On the screen, Diana started walking for the door, then suddenly turned around. Reed turned up the sound.

"What did you say?" Diana's voice sounded tinny, like a distant echo on the tape, but her words were clear.

"He took her last night. After stopping in at your sister's wedding reception to pay his respects."

"The Copycat Killer?"

"Of course."

"How do you know this?"

"I know a lot of things, Diana. Like the desperation a parent feels when kept away from a child. Especially when she needs you most. I could tell you all about it if you would visit me."

He stopped the tape, freezing Kane and Diana on the screen. "Is that the part you meant?"

She nodded. "Do you think I'm just reading into what he said?"

"Maybe. But the location of the Laundromat is enough reason to check it out." Switching off the television and removing the tape, he strode to his desk and plucked his suit jacket from the back of his chair. "Nikki, call me if any more reports come in."

"Will do."

"And keep trying to find Meredith Unger. I

realize it's Sunday, but it seems damn suspicious she picked today to fall off the edge of the earth."

"I'll find her."

Reed glanced at Perreth. "We wait on the press."

Perreth glowered in answer.

Reed didn't seem to notice. His focus skimmed over Perreth and landed on Diana. "You're coming with me."

DIANA SETTLED HERSELF into the passenger seat of Reed's sedan, secured the seat belt across her chest and peered out the bug-spattered windshield. "So what were you and Perreth discussing in there?"

Reed shifted the car into gear. Eyes glued to the road ahead, he merged with traffic flowing a block off the capitol square, but instead of turning down East Washington Avenue and heading for Nadine Washburn's east-side home, he kept going, circling the state capitol grounds.

Diana dug her fingers into the car's armrest. "Reed? Where are we going?" When he had asked her to go with him, she'd assumed he was taking her to question Nadine's mother. It was beginning to look as though she should have remembered the old saying about assuming making an ass of you and me.

"*You're* going to the hotel where Sylvie and Bryce are staying. They booked you a room adjoining theirs. An officer is posted in the hall. You'll be safe there."

"I'd be safe with Nikki at the station."

"Yes, you and Nikki and the reporters I'm sure Perreth will try to convince the lieutenant to call as soon as I stepped out the door."

"You think he would do that?"

Reed raised a brow.

"Okay, so he *would* do that."

"We've been lucky to keep the fact that you and Sylvie are Kane's daughters out of the press so far. With the copycat active again, that luck isn't likely to hold. Especially with Perreth chomping at the bit for media exposure. Exposure that would get his name in the papers and hurt you—and by extension me—at the same time."

Great. Media exposure would turn her and Sylvie's lives upside down. Her head ached just thinking about it. "So what do we do?"

"Put the media storm off for as long as possible. And hope we catch the copycat. Soon."

"So I should be helping. Not hiding."

"You should be lying low. And that's just what you're going to do."

Lying low. Staying safe. Reed's answer to everything where she was concerned. "I need to see Nadine Washburn's mother. I need to talk to her.

If it wasn't for Kane forcing me to visit, her daughter wouldn't have been sucked into the nightmare she's in now."

"Listen to yourself." Reed glanced at her, his nearly black eyes sharp. "You're doing just what Kane wants you to do. He'll threaten you and Sylvie and innocent women washing their clothing and anyone else he thinks will give him control over you. So unless you're planning to take responsibility for the whole human race, it might be more advantageous to focus on your visit with him tomorrow rather than beating yourself up."

She took a deep cool breath. He was right, as much as she hated admitting it. She needed to put her energy where she could have the greatest chance of stopping the copycat.

And Kane.

"So how am I supposed to focus on tomorrow while I'm sequestered in a hotel?"

"You're supposed to rest, maybe even eat something."

Fat chance of that. She didn't feel the least bit hungry. And although she was exhausted, she knew she'd never be able to fall asleep. Not tonight. But maybe there was another way she could prepare herself for tomorrow's meeting with Kane. "We're going to my apartment first, right?"

"Your apartment?" He shook his head. "I want you safe at the hotel, not in an apartment that isn't security locked."

"I need clothing, maybe a toothbrush and some other stuff. Don't you think?"

He ran a hand over his face. "I suppose. Sure." He made a turn and pointed the car in the direction of her apartment.

Diana leaned back against the headrest. Clothes and a toothbrush would be nice, but it was the other stuff she was most anxious to pick up. She'd done a lot of research into serial killers and Dryden Kane after she'd learned he was her biological father. She'd even gone so far as to insinuate herself into a study the university was conducting on Kane—a study directed by Professor Bertram, the man who had nearly murdered her in his quest for revenge against Dryden Kane. But while she'd worked with Bertram interviewing Kane, she'd squirreled away copies of every paper and note she'd been able to get her hands on. Copies she still had in the storage locker of her apartment building. Since Reed wanted her to prepare for tomorrow, he could hardly complain about hauling a couple of file boxes to the hotel along with her suitcase.

Reed swung the car to the curb outside the front entrance of Diana's apartment. He switched off the ignition and they both climbed out into the humid June air, scents of moist earth and plant life thick from last night's heavy rain.

She turned to him as he climbed from the car. "I might need your help carrying some stuff."

"What are you planning to bring?" Reed circled the car and stepped to the curb beside her.

"If you don't want to help carry it, you can wait in the car."

He shot her a dry look. "Follow me."

Stifling a sigh, she fell in behind him, walking up the sidewalk and into the lobby. Once inside, he made her wait at the door while he scrutinized every inch of the modest lobby, as if he expected a man with a gun to crawl from under the vinyl bench or pop out of one of the tiny locked mailboxes that lined the wall.

"You really think this is necessary?"

He didn't answer. Instead, he paused at the door to the stairwell and stared at the mud-tracked entry rug.

"What are you looking for?"

"Nothing. That's just an unusual tread pattern." He pointed at mud shaped in a wavy pattern staining the rug.

Apparently he was going to micromanage every second of her life. Even to the point of analyzing dirty rugs. "So? It poured last night."

"But where does someone find that much mud around here?"

He had a point. The area around the apartment was covered with a lush June lawn and fresh layer of mulch in the flower beds. For the first summer in years, the street out front wasn't torn up with construction. But while mud in the entry did seem a little odd, it still didn't require a news bulletin. Of course, knowing Reed, he was probably just trying to frighten her. Impress on her the danger she faced if she insisted on staying at her apartment.

As if that were necessary.

Finished with the mud, he started up the stairs.

"Wait," she said. "I need to get my suitcase and some other stuff from my storage locker."

"The other stuff again. It had better not be too heavy." Changing course, Reed led her down the steps into the dank coolness of the basement. He stopped at the secured door leading to the lockers for her section of the building. "Keys?"

At one time, he'd had his own. Blocking those days from her mind, Diana dug into her purse.

Down the hall, a door opened. Diana's next-door neighbor, Louis Ingersoll, stepped out of the laundry room, hoisting a basket of clothes. As soon as he spotted Reed, his eyes narrowed. His contempt reached down the hall like a cold draft.

Diana shook her head. Explaining all that had

happened to Louis was the last thing she needed. He'd been her friend in the months before her wedding, watching her apartment when she was away, clipping stories about Dryden Kane from the newspaper after he'd learned of her involvement in the research project. But since she'd broken up with Reed, their friendship had taken on an uncomfortable edge.

Or maybe she just hadn't noticed his romantic expectations until then. "Hey, Louis."

Louis didn't take his glare from Reed. A flush spread up his freckled neck, turning his face as red as his hair. "Is there anything I can help with?"

"Detective McCaskey is here in an official capacity." She shouldn't feel compelled to explain— whether Reed was here or not wasn't Louis's business—but she couldn't stand that look in his eyes. As if Reed were his enemy. As if Diana had betrayed him. She'd never meant to lead him on, but obviously that was what she'd done.

"What do you mean, an official capacity? Did something happen?"

"Nothing you have to worry about," Reed said, words clipped.

Diana shot him a quelling look. Reed had never been fond of Louis. No doubt she'd been the only one blind to Louis's crush. A situation remedied when he'd given her a necklace of emeralds and diamond chips for Christmas—a necklace he refused to take back.

Even now he glanced down at her throat, as if noticing her lack of jewelry, even though she'd never once worn his gift. "If there's anything I can do, Diana, you let me know."

"Thanks." Fingertips hitting metal, she fished her keys out of her purse and handed them to Reed. She couldn't wait to end this uncomfortable exchange. "We'll talk later, okay, Louis?"

"I'll be here."

Reed pushed the storage-room door open, and they slipped inside, clearing the hall for Louis to pass with his laundry basket.

She let out a breath of relief.

"So he still hasn't given up, huh?"

"Louis is my friend."

"He might be your friend, but you are his obsession."

She didn't want to talk about it. The air was charged enough between her and Reed without introducing pointless jealousy into the mix.

She stepped past him and faced the rows of wood and chicken wire that formed individual storage lockers lining the walls. Snagging the keys from his hand, she strode to her locker and opened the padlock that secured the door. She'd been meaning to sort through the jumble of boxes jamming the space, but with Sylvie's wedding and move to Madison, Diana's last semester of grad school and the fact that she hadn't been ready to deal with much of anything the past few months, she hadn't been down here since Christmas.

A gossamer strand of spiderweb tickled her face. Wiping it clear, she moved several boxes before she came to the suitcase. And the pair of file boxes underneath.

Her heart stuttered in her chest.

After her experience with Professor Bertram, she hadn't been able to look at the files she'd compiled. She'd merely shoveled the material into the file boxes and stacked them down here. The thought of sharing the same living space with them, many of which had notes written in Bertram's hand, repulsed her.

She jingled the key chain in her hand. Suddenly she didn't want to see those papers again. Just the thought of them brought back memories of that cabin, the darkness, the burn of the ropes on her wrists, her eventual loss of hope, of strength.

"You want those boxes?" he asked.

"I'm going to take some work with me to the hotel, too, if you don't mind." She could feel his skepticism without turning to look at his face.

"Fine with me."

She bent over the first box, wrestling it out of the pile.

"What's inside?"

"Papers," she answered, hoping he wouldn't probe further, yet knowing he would.

"Papers having something to do with Dryden Kane?"

She let the box plunk back to the floor. She might as well tell him her intentions. "I'm going to read through my notes from previous interviews with him. Prepare for tomorrow."

"Is this the 'other stuff' you needed?"

"Yes."

"What did you think? That if you told me what was really in the box, I'd take them?"

She gave him a look, not bothering to state the obvious.

He stroked his chin. "Your lack of trust in me is stunning." Leaning down, he hoisted the box she'd just dropped and carried it out of the locker.

She pulled the other box out and slid it across the cement floor until it rested beside her suitcase.

The room plunged to blackness.

Chapter Five

Adrenaline jolted Diana's bloodstream. She strained her eyes, trying to see something. Anything but colored spots swimming in endless blackness. "What happened?"

"Shh." Reed's suit jacket rustled. A click sounded off the cement, the sound of him unsnapping his holster and pulling out his gun.

Diana's heart slammed high in her chest. Had someone cut the electricity on purpose? Someone like the Copycat Killer? Reed seemed to think so.

Her legs began to shake. Silence hung in the dank air, heavy enough to choke her.

"Where are the circuit breakers?" Reed whispered.

Diana never had a reason to know. She combed her mind, trying to picture where she might have seen something like that. "I think I remember some electrical boxes in the laundry room."

Reed's shoes scraped lightly in the darkness, moving toward the door. Moving out into the hall. He couldn't leave her. Not in here. Not in the darkness.

Where the killer could be waiting.

No, the killer wasn't in here. He couldn't be. But he might be out in the hall. Out in the hall waiting for Reed.

Panic flared hot in her chest. She pushed herself up from her crouch, willing her trembling knees to support her. Gripping the cage of chicken wire, she felt her way to the two-by-fours framing the locker door.

"Stay in the locker," Reed whispered.

"But—"

"I don't want to have to worry about where you are."

Of course. What was she thinking? That she was going to save Reed? How? She had no gun. She had no weapon of any kind. And although she'd started attending classes on self-defense, at this moment she didn't know if she could stand let alone remember a single move.

She backed into the storage locker and lowered herself into an uneasy squat. The darkness closed around her, as heavy and oppressive as a blanket. A pall. She struggled to hear above the pound of her pulse.

It was torture, waiting like this. Not knowing what was happening. Helpless. Images exploded in front of her eyes, memory playing out against the black screen. She remembered every excruciating moment of the days and nights she'd lain tied in that dark cabin. The burn of the ropes against her wrists. The terrible thirst that parched her mouth and throat. The emptiness that opened like a chasm inside her.

She couldn't push it out of her mind.

She'd been worried about Reed then, too. She'd seen Professor Bertram hit him with the tire iron. She'd seen the way his head had bounced against the tile floor. She'd seen the blood.

And she'd been helpless to do anything to help him. The helplessness was the worst. It ate into her until there was nothing left but bitter darkness.

A sound came from out in the hall.

She couldn't sit here and wait for Reed to be attacked. Wait for the killer to find her. Wait to relive horrors she'd barely survived the first time.

She groped in the darkness until her hands touched the cardboard flaps of boxes. There must be something here, something she could use to defend herself, to help Reed.

She pulled the flaps of one box open. Taking a breath of dusty air, she shoved a hand inside. Her fingers brushed the spines of books. She tried another box, her hand plunging into soft fall sweaters. Her third try, the buttery leather of a softball glove. She clawed deeper. Something cold and curved and as smooth as brushed metal met her palm. She gripped the softball bat and pulled it from the box as quietly as she could.

It felt good in her hands. Solid. Strong. She focused on the locker door. If something happened, if someone came inside, she could take a swing at him. She could defend herself.

The trembling in her legs spread through her whole body. Her breathing roared in her ears, yet oxygen never seemed to make it to her lungs.

Oh, God, don't let this happen again.

The lights flickered, then held.

She blinked, the sudden illumination blinding. Relief rushed through her bloodstream, relief she was afraid to feel.

Footsteps sounded in the hall.

She tightened her grip on the bat.

Reed stepped around the corner.

She let the bat clatter to the floor.

"Diana." He rushed to her side, encircling her with his arms, holding her on her feet.

Her body dissolved, as if the muscle holding her upright had turned to quivering goo. "Who was it?"

"I don't know. But I'm getting you out of here. I'll come back for the boxes when backup arrives."

"And Nadine Washburn's mother?" Reed had planned to talk to the woman about her daughter's disappearance. But right now, the last thing Diana wanted was for him to leave her alone.

"I'll have another detective do it. Don't worry. I'm not going anywhere just now."

She nodded, but she didn't move. The way she was shaking, she didn't know if her legs would carry her. Worse, she didn't want to leave the protection of Reed's arms.

BY THE TIME THE OTHER OFFICERS arrived, Diana had gotten her shaking under control, but the tide of failure sweeping through her wasn't so easy to stem.

She'd tried so hard. To stand on her own. To be strong. And yet, she hadn't been with Reed ten hours and any progress she'd made over the past months had washed away, leaving her clinging and shaking in his arms.

She leaned against Reed's car and waited for him and the other officers to complete their sweep of the building. The only thing she could think to do was pray the circuit breaker flicking off was an overloaded circuit. If it was more than that, she didn't know what she'd do.

"Diana?" Reed walked toward her. A small gift bag dangled from his fingers. He crossed the sidewalk and stopped in front of her. "Who would have left you a gift?"

Diana stared at the package, her mind a blank. "I don't know."

"I might." He stepped past her and reached for the car door.

"What is it?"

"You can see it later."

The tremor reignited, rippling through her legs. "It's from the copycat, isn't it?"

Reed opened the driver's door.

She grabbed his arm. "Isn't it?"

His bicep hardened under her palm. "You can see it later. You're in no condition now."

"I need to see it now." She pressed back the tears flooding her eyes. She couldn't cry. She couldn't let the emotions surging through her overwhelm her. Not unless she wanted to prove Reed's point. That she couldn't handle the truth. That she might never be strong enough to stand on her own. "Please."

He looked down at her, searching as if he could see her thoughts written across her face. Slowly, he dipped a hand into his jacket and pulled out a pair of plastic gloves like the ones he was wearing. "It's not the type of surface that is likely to give us good prints, but it pays to be careful."

She pulled the gloves on. Drawing a deep breath, she opened the bag and peered inside.

A small box nestled in the bag. The fading twilight gleamed on its white skin. She looked to Reed. "What is it?"

"A music box."

Cold skittered up her spine. Memories niggled at the back of her mind, memories she couldn't quite grasp. "Can I touch it?"

"Are you sure you want to do this?"

She wasn't sure. She wasn't sure at all. She managed a nod.

Holding a handle in each hand, he spread the bag open so she could pull out the box.

Covered in white satin and fluffy tulle, the tiny box looked like a wedding favor. Or a little girl's dream.

She grasped the box in one hand and caught the tiny clasp with the edge of her fingernail, flipping it open. She held her breath as she lifted the lid.

Pink satin lined the box, a mirror fitted inside the lid. And in front of the mirror, a tiny bride twirled, her dress and veil frothing around her like frosting on a wedding cake. A metallic tune tickled the air.

Diana didn't remember her childhood before age three. Not really. Only bits and pieces. A feeling here. An isolated image there. But there was no mistaking the song plucked out by the music box's metallic tines.

"'The Wedding March.'" Her voice rasped hoarsely in her ears, a voice she hardly knew. But she knew exactly who'd given her this gift. She could feel the shiver of memory in each metallic note. "It's from him. It's from Dryden Kane."

Chapter Six

Reed stopped his sedan at the curb outside the downtown hotel Sylvie and Bryce had chosen and glanced at Diana. Night had fallen while he and several other officers had been busy turning Diana's apartment building upside down looking for evidence the Copycat Killer—or whoever had delivered Kane's gift—had left behind. Despite the passage of time and thick shadows veiling her face, Diana looked as pale and shell-shocked as she had after opening that damn music box.

He blew a breath through tight lips and switched off the ignition. He'd known dealing with Diana would be painful, but he'd never guessed how bad it would get. At least this morning he could muster some anger toward her, some bitterness for breaking their engagement and his heart. But now he didn't even have that defense. Now all he could think about was keeping her safe.

Checking traffic, he opened the door and climbed out. The sooner he got her checked into the hotel and away from him, the better. It wouldn't remove her from his thoughts, but at least she wouldn't be by his side, his old feelings chafing like a pair of ill-fitting shoes too expensive to throw away.

She joined him as he opened the trunk. He grasped her suitcase, and set it on the curb and reached up to close the trunk.

"What about my notes on Kane?"

The notes. Damn. He was hoping she would have forgotten the notes. Spending the night reading about the horrors that monster had committed was the last thing she needed. "I need to make copies. I have to be sure we didn't miss something."

"So make copies. *Tomorrow.*"

He probably should argue with her, but he didn't have the heart. He glanced at his watch. Already ten o'clock. It had taken far longer than he'd ever imagined to sweep Diana's building and canvass her neighbors. Even after all the hours they'd been there, and on a Sunday night, they hadn't been able to talk to everyone. Like Louis Ingersoll. The little redheaded worm had disappeared sometime after they'd seen him in the basement. Not that Reed wouldn't catch up with him. "We could make copies right now," Diana said, bringing his attention crashing back to the boxes in the trunk.

He eyed the boxes. It would take an hour or more to copy all those files. Another hour of being with Diana. Of wanting to take care of her, protect her. Of wanting her to be his own.

Maybe Perreth was right. Maybe another detective should deal with Diana.

He shook his head. He just needed some time away. If he was really considering Perreth's ideas, he must be too tired to think. "Okay. I'll have someone copy them in the morning."

Trying not to notice the satisfied press of Diana's lips, he lugged the boxes into the hotel. He placed them on a bellboy's cart while Diana checked in, then they wheeled their way into an elevator and through a hall to her room. Reaching the room, Reed greeted Officer Kuklin outside in the hall, tipped the bellboy, and prepared to make his exit.

A knock sounded on the door leading to the adjoining room.

"Sylvie." Diana raced to the door and pulled it open.

Sylvie opened her arms and engulfed her sister in a hug. "I'm so glad you're here. I can't believe you saw Kane. Why didn't you tell me that's what you were going to do?"

"Because you would have stopped me."

"You bet I would have."

Bryce appeared behind his bride, watching the sisters, concern threading across his brow.

Reed stepped toward the door. With Bryce here and the officers outside, Diana would be safe. Reed could work off some tension on his weight bench and get back to concentrating on the case. With the Copycat Killer active again, his rest would have to come in the form of fifteen-minute naps. Giving Bryce a nod, he strode for the door.

"Reed, wait," Bryce called. "Someone left a gift for Sylvie at the hotel's registration desk. It's something you should see."

He turned around and stared at the little white music box cradled in Bryce's hands.

DIANA'S HEART SANK into her stomach. She stared at the white box identical to the one Reed had sent to the crime lab.

"We thought it was from you," Sylvie said. "Your wedding gift."

Diana could kick herself. "He sent me one, too. I should have called to warn you." The most disturbing thing was that the music box had been delivered to the hotel. And that meant the copycat knew where Sylvie was. "I bought you four place settings and a bud vase."

Sylvie tried to smile, but the attempt fell flat.

She looked as pale and drawn as she had this morning. No doubt she hadn't rested all day. And maybe she hadn't been able to eat either. "Kane mentioned a music box to me, back when you disappeared last fall."

Reed stepped away from the door and joined them in Sylvie and Bryce's room. "What did he say?"

"That Diana loved a puppet when she was a kid. And we both loved a music box."

Bryce nodded. "It should be on the videotape."

Reed scribbled something in a notebook.

"It plays the 'Wedding March'?"

Sylvie cracked open the lid and the march tinkled through the room like the sound of shattering glass. Shuddering, she closed the box. "I have to sit down."

Sylvie perched on the edge of the bed, looking as if she might need to dash to the bathroom any moment.

Diana looked down at the bloody edges of Sylvie's fingernails. A habit she'd had as a child, Sylvie had begun digging at the edges of her nails after coming face-to-face with Kane last fall. As hard as the reality of having a serial killer for a father was on Diana, it was tougher for Sylvie. She'd spent her life longing to know her biological parents only to find out her father was a serial killer.

Diana covered Sylvie's hands with hers. "Go on

your honeymoon. Concentrate on that baby you're going to have. Concentrate on Bryce. They're your family. Don't think about Kane."

Sylvie shook her head. "And leave you here to deal with this alone? Not a chance."

"I'm not alone." She glanced in Reed's direction before she could catch herself. Shaking her head, she looked back to Sylvie. "Besides, it's my fault he's in our lives to begin with. I need to deal with it."

Sylvie shook her head. "We've been through that."

"Yes. And nothing's changed."

"This is me, Diana. Kane is my father as much as he is yours." Sylvie was trying to put on a brave face, but Diana couldn't help but notice her flinch when she said the words.

"He can't know you're pregnant."

Sylvie jerked her head up. "What do you think he'd do?"

"I don't know. But we don't want to find out."

Sylvie rubbed a palm over her still-flat belly.

An ache hollowed out in Diana's own belly. An ache of longing and fear she didn't want to own. "The surest way to keep him from finding out is to go away. At least until the police can identify the Copycat Killer."

"She's right, Sylvie." Reed's voice came from behind Diana, smoothing over her like a caress. "You need to go. You have a lot to lose."

"We all have a lot to lose." Sylvie zeroed in on Reed. "How close are you to finding him?"

"Not close enough."

Sylvie sat back on the bed with a little sigh, as if she'd reached a decision. "I can't just sit around and pretend to vacation while you face that monster down alone, Diana."

Diana shook her head. Sylvie couldn't stay here. There had to be something she could say to convince her to go, something that would convince her not to put herself and her baby in danger for Diana's sake. But what?

"What if you could be a bigger help out of town than you are here?" Reed looked from Sylvie to Bryce.

"How?" Bryce asked.

"Kane has some sort of connection to this copycat. Could be a recent connection, could be someone he knew in the past. We're expending a lot of resources looking into everyone he's come into contact with recently."

"But in the past?"

"We've run into a dead end there."

Bryce lowered himself on to the bed beside Sylvie and took his wife's hand in his. "And you think *we* might be able to help?"

"How would you two feel about taking your honeymoon to Oshishobee, Wisconsin?"

"Oshishobee?" Sylvie asked. "Where's that?"

"It's northeast, on the way to the Upper Peninsula." Diana knew the town, though she'd never been there. She also thought she knew where Reed was leading. "It's where Kane grew up."

"Nikki and I went up there last fall," Reed said. "But it's a very tight-lipped small town. I'm willing to bet people who refused to cooperate with the police might be more open to talking to one of Kane's daughters."

Sylvie looked up at Bryce.

"What would we be looking for specifically?" Bryce asked.

"Today Kane mentioned something about the Copycat Killer being like a son to him."

Bryce raised his brows. "You think Kane has a son? And the copycat might be him?"

"Hard to say. He might be someone younger that Kane knew, someone who looked up to him. Or someone he bullied. Of course his connection to the copycat might not have anything to do with his past. But we can't afford not to look into every possibility."

Sylvie tilted her head skeptically. "With all that was written about Kane, *someone* must have researched his life growing up."

"Oshishobee has a Native American name, but it's a tight-knit Norwegian town. People don't trust any strangers, not just police detectives from Madison. I'm hoping as Kane's daughter, you can cut through some of that resistance."

Diana held her breath, afraid to say anything that might interfere.

Sylvie looked up at her husband. She pressed her lips into a determined line. "I think we'd better pack."

Diana expelled the breath she was holding in a whoosh.

"But I'm worried about you, Diana. I don't like the thought of you seeing him again, let alone meeting him every day. If Bryce and I agree to go, the two of you have to make me a deal."

An uneasy feeling clamped down on Diana's shoulders. "What?"

"You need to stick together. Reed, you're the only one I trust to keep my sister safe."

A muscle twitched along Reed's jaw.

Diana forced a smile to her lips that she was far from feeling. As if she'd had any choice in the matter in the first place. "You know Reed, Syl. He'll watch over my every move."

REED ACCOMPANIED DIANA BACK to her room, giving Sylvie and Bryce a chance to talk and make plans for their trip. But although Diana was grateful Reed had convinced Sylvie to leave town, being alone with Reed was the last thing she wanted at the moment. The promise Sylvie had elicited from them—that Reed would watch over Diana while Sylvie and Bryce were gone—hung heavy in the air like humidity gathering before a thunderstorm.

Diana cleared her throat. She had to set things straight. The last thing she needed was for Reed to feel even more responsible for her than he already did. If that was even possible. "Don't worry about what Sylvie said. What she wanted us to promise."

He looked up at her, startled, as if she'd disturbed him from an engrossing thought. "That I'll keep you safe?"

She shook her head. She knew he'd do that regardless. "That we need to stick together."

"Oh, that. Don't worry. I know it isn't personal." He was clearly making fun of her. But there was no humor in his voice.

She couldn't blame him. There was nothing funny about this situation. Nothing at all. Being around Reed today had made her feel empty and vulnerable and raw. And he didn't seem to be faring much better.

He walked toward the door and laid a hand on the knob. But instead of pulling it open, he turned back to face her. "You know, Sylvie isn't the only one in danger here."

Of course she knew that. "All the women in the Madison area are in danger."

"You should get out of town, too."

She held up a hand. They'd been through this before, his need to protect her, to take care of her, to control everything that happened in her life. "I don't need to hear this again."

"Everything both you and I said to Sylvie also applies to you."

"Except the pregnancy." She hoped the last bit would add some levity. It fell far short.

She folded her arms around her middle. She hadn't eaten all day, yet she didn't feel hungry. If anything, the nervous vibration in her stomach made her feel as sick as Sylvie had looked.

She drew in a deep breath and forced confidence into her voice. "I'm in a position to talk to Kane, to understand the way he thinks, maybe even to find out who the copycat is and where he is holding Nadine Washburn. I can't leave. You of all people know that."

"You have a very optimistic view of what Kane is going to let you learn."

"Optimistic?" She threw up her hands and let them land against her thighs with a stinging smack. "I don't know if he's going to tell me anything. But we have to use what we can get, don't we?"

"Within reason."

"Reason? What is reasonable? Or maybe you should ask Nadine Washburn's mother that question."

"If Nadine has been abducted by the copycat, I want to save her every bit as much as you do."

"I don't doubt that."

"Then what's your point?"

"I know what it's like to be tied to a bed in the darkness, waiting to die. I know what she's thinking. I know what she's feeling. I'm the only one in this room who truly understands what's within reason and what isn't."

Reed's face went rigid. "I understand perfectly. I was there when you were kidnapped, remember? I might not know what Nadine feels, but I more than understand the pain her mother is living through. I understand the worry. I understand the helplessness. I understand the guilt."

"Guilt?" Obviously somewhere in his last monologue, Reed had stopped talking about Nadine's mother and started describing himself. "Why on earth would *you* feel guilty? Vincent Bertram nearly killed you."

He shook his head slowly, his black eyes boring into her. "Bertram was nothing. Losing *you* nearly killed me."

The weight of his look solidified and sank into her chest. "Reed, don't."

"Why the hell not? I'm sick of pretending that you breaking off our marriage was good for both of us. I'm sick of pretending seeing you again is just business, just part of my job. Ever since you walked into that damn diner this morning, all I can think about is how I shouldn't be seeing the way you brush your hair from your cheek or hearing that tremble in your voice when you're frightened. Or your scent…God, I certainly shouldn't be leaning toward you every chance I get just to breathe you in."

She turned away from him. She wanted him to stop. He had to stop. She couldn't hear this.

"Damn it, Diana. When you're around, I can't see anything but you."

"Then why did you insist on going with me? Why didn't you let Nikki handle my meeting with Kane? Or, God help me, even Perreth?"

"You haven't heard anything I've said, have you?"

On the contrary, she'd heard every word, every hitch in his voice, every loaded pause. She could feel the intensity of them vibrating in her bones. "I've heard enough to know we shouldn't be together."

His footsteps sounded behind her. He gripped her arm and turned her to face him. "Losing you once almost killed me. Losing you, to Kane, to the damn copycat…"

His face was so close, she could reach out her

hand and trace the line of dark stubble on his cheek. She could lean forward, just a little, and find herself in his arms.

"It's not going to happen. And the only way I can make sure it doesn't is to be next to you when he tries."

She looked down, unable to peer into his eyes one second longer. She'd been an idiot to think anything between her and Reed wouldn't be personal. Looking at him across a crowded room would be personal.

But where did that leave her? Where did it leave them both? "I can't go back, Reed. You say you almost lost me, well I lost myself long before our wedding day." That is, if she'd ever found herself in the first place.

She could feel his gaze on her, his eyes searching, struggling to understand.

She didn't know if she could help him. Not any more than she'd been able to when she'd given back his ring. She wasn't sure she understood any of this herself.

Taking a deep breath, she met his eyes. She had to try. It was only fair to him that she try. "I've always been what other people wanted. My mother. My father."

Reed's face grew hard, as if he sensed what was coming.

"You."

His eyes darkened, as if bruised. "I never asked you to be anything but who you are."

She longed to run her hand along his cheek, to smooth away the hurt, to take back the words. But she couldn't let herself. She had to tell him the truth. At least the small part of it she had figured out.

She took a step to the side, putting a little more distance between them, hoping it would help her think. "I know you never asked me to be what you wanted. You never even told me what you wanted. Not in words. You didn't have to. I sensed it. I gave you what you were looking for before you even knew you wanted it."

He shook his head. "We were happy together. We loved each other."

"I loved you."

"But you don't believe I loved you?" His expression didn't change, but anger sharpened the edges of his voice.

"I never gave you the chance. I never even let you know who I really was. I was afraid to."

"Afraid? Why?" He took a step toward her, closing the distance between them. "I didn't do anything to make you afraid."

"I didn't say you did, Reed. It's me. It's who I am. It's what I do. I make myself what others want me to be."

He watched her under lowered brows. Back to the bedside lamp, his eyes blended with shadow.

She couldn't tell if he was following her or not, but she had to push on. She had to make him see. "I didn't even know I was doing it until I was tied up in that dark cabin waiting to die. I had to draw on myself to survive. On the strength inside me." She closed her eyes. The room spun out of control. Just like the days and nights in the cabin. The raw vulnerability. The fear. "Reed, there was nothing for me to draw on. There was nothing there."

He touched her arm, sending chills racing along her nerves. "You were frightened out of your mind, Diana. Anyone would feel that way."

"No. You would never feel that way, Reed. You know who you are. You know where your strength lies."

"I'm a detective. I have training to fall back on. It's not the same thing."

"Sylvie didn't feel that way. Bryce didn't feel that way. If they had, we'd all be dead."

"You're being too hard on yourself."

"I'm being realistic. I'm not hiding from the truth anymore." She forced her mind closed, shutting out the sensation of his fingers on her skin. "My adoptive father dictated how I should feel, how I should think."

"Ed Gale was an abusive ass. *I* never dictated anything."

"No. You didn't. You rescued me. You fixed things for me. You took care of me."

"And how is that bad? That's how a man *should* treat the woman he loves."

Loves. Not *loved.* As if she had to wonder how he still felt about her. Or at least, how he felt about his *idea* of her.

"I have to learn to rescue myself. I have to take care of myself." That wasn't quite right. She tried again, groping through her mind for an emotion just out of her grasp. "No, I have to feel like there's a me inside worth rescuing. A me that isn't dictated by my need to please others. A core me. I know this makes no sense to you. You've always known who you are. It doesn't even make sense to me, really. But if I ever face a tough situation again, I need something to draw on. Something inside *me*. I need to know I can pull myself through."

Darkness seeped into his eyes. Tension pulled his lips into a scowl.

Her throat ached. She was doing a horrible job of explaining, but she didn't know a way to make her feelings more clear. If only he could understand how she wanted to kiss that scowl away, curl up in his arms and forget all the questions and insecurities and shadowy emotions ripping her apart. He was the only man she'd ever wanted, the only man she'd ever loved. But she knew in every fiber of her being that for her, he was the wrong man. "You'll always take care of me, Reed. It's who you are. And as long as I'm with you, I'll never learn to rely on myself. I'll never really know who I am."

She turned away, toward the window. The drapes' multiple colors blurred through burgeoning tears. Tilting her head back, she opened her eyes wide and tried to will them back. She wouldn't let herself cry. She couldn't. She'd already poured out too much.

"Okay." His voice cut her thoughts like a laser.

"Okay?"

"What can I do to help?"

Swallowing into an aching throat, she turned back to face him, trying to read those shadowed eyes.

"I meant what I said about not losing you to Kane. I'm not going to stay away from you. But if I can do anything short of that…"

The breath she pulled into her lungs seared all the way to her toes. She wasn't sure what she'd expected him to say, to do. But she hadn't expected this. "Thank you."

He raked a hand through his hair before dropping it to his side. He looked around the room, as if he didn't know what to do next, as if he didn't even recognize where he was. "You're going to have to help me here. You're going to have to tell me what you need."

She willed her voice to function. "You can let me do more than make coffee. Let me help with the investigation. At least as much as I'm able."

He nodded.

"You can stop shielding me from unpleasant things. I need to know what we're up against."

"Okay."

"And you can stop worrying about me."

"I can't promise you that."

"Maybe that's a little too much to ask." She gave him a half smile. "But have some faith in me, okay?"

He stepped toward her. The light from the lamp illuminated his face, showing eyes dark with emotion, with sincerity. "That's something I *can* promise."

Diana's vision blurred once again. Those words shouldn't mean so much to her. They couldn't. But somehow, despite everything, they meant the world.

Chapter Seven

The moonlight glowed blue on her naked white skin as she ran across the clearing. It was a good light for her. Hid the cellulite and the stretch marks. Smoothed over her hips. It even made her breasts look, if not perky, at least not so saggy.

He raised the rifle to his shoulder and lined her up in the sights. He'd played with the first three. Toyed with them. Stalked them. He didn't feel like playing this time.

Maybe it was because he'd waited so long. The fantasies had burned inside him like a hunger until all that mattered was filling his belly. Maybe it was because she was older, and the dreams of killing his mother, exciting at first, left him limp in the end. Maybe it was because she'd laughed at him.

But whatever the reason, this one had been a disappointment.

She raced for the brush. He had to admit, her fear

gave him a charge. And standing here, resting his finger on the trigger, he was as hard as a tree branch.

Look who was laughing now.

He squeezed the trigger. The air cracked. The rifle kicked sweetly against his shoulder. He watched her lurch and fall as the perfume of gunpowder spiced the air.

He strode across the clearing toward her. He'd gotten a clean shot. He'd taken out one of her legs, just as he'd been instructed. As he approached, he could hear her thrashing, trying to crawl the rest of the way to the forest's edge, to safety.

There was no safety for her.

He pulled his knife from the sheath on his belt. He wrapped his fingers around the handle, the charge of excitement starting to pulse through his body. He'd follow instructions for the kill, too. Pushing the knife in just under her ribs. Letting her screams wash over him like a refreshing rain. Watching the life drain from her eyes as he pulled the blade down through her belly. Next he would clean her out, warm and sticky on his hands.

Then he'd wait to find out what he was supposed to do with the body.

He looked down at the fear shining in her eyes. He listened to the whimper dying on her lips.

As thrilling as he knew killing her would be, he couldn't help wishing for more, wanting more.

With each of his murders, he'd learned so much. About death and life. About the strength and power in himself. About hunger. But it wasn't enough. He'd been acting a part, following Dryden Kane's instructions, playing out Dryden Kane's fantasies. But now he could feel his own desires building. They pressed against the inside of his skull, until he felt he'd explode with lust.

There was something *he* wanted. Something blond and beautiful with light blue eyes and perky breasts. And soon, very soon, he would reach out and pluck it like ripe fruit off a tree. He would bite into her, devour her, and let the juice run sticky down his chin.

And no one could stop him. Not Reed McCaskey. Not even Dryden Kane.

Chapter Eight

By the time Reed, Diana and Nikki reached the north Madison district office, Reed had successfully pushed the emotional turmoil of the night before into a dark closet in the back of his mind. At least he hoped he had. He'd already spent hours dwelling on what Diana had said—time he should have spent focusing one hundred percent on the copycat case and today's visit to Dryden Kane. By the time he'd finished half of what he'd hoped to accomplish, he'd already run out of time for even a short nap in his cramped and smelly cubicle.

Oh, well, he could sleep when he was dead.

Diana had been wrong last night, about a number of things. For one, he *did* know her. He knew how smart she was, knew the different tones of her laughs, and the way she doted on her sister. He also knew she was as tough as they came. She hadn't had it easy. Not with her bastard of an adoptive father, not dealing with a mother who, though she was perfectly healthy, was as demanding and weak as an invalid. And after witnessing her pain last night, he knew he loved her more than ever. He just hoped it was enough to enable him to stand back and let her handle things on her own.

He led Nikki and Diana down a hall and to the conference room he'd asked to have set aside. He glanced at Diana. She looked so determined, marching down the hall, so fresh and young, dressed in a simple T-shirt and jeans. But the way she'd kept touching the delicate heart necklace she'd gotten from Sylvie revealed just how insecure she felt. About her future and her sister's.

He hadn't told Diana what he'd arranged last night after he'd left her hotel room. He'd hardly had time to tell Nikki. But he figured she'd be pleased. "We have a visitor." He slowed his stride, allowing her to catch up.

"A visitor?"

"Trent Burnell from Quantico."

"The FBI agent who profiled Kane?"

He should have figured she'd know who Burnell was. Judging from the weight of those file boxes he'd hauled to her hotel room last night, she must have compiled everything there was to know about Dryden Kane. And the man who had captured

Kane, not once but twice, loomed large in the serial killer's history. "I got hold of Burnell last night. He was flying to the west coast today to give a lecture, but he agreed to make a pit stop on the way." Now he hoped Burnell's plane was on time and an officer had remembered to pick him up from the airport.

Diana tilted her head to look at him. "He's here to work the copycat case? I thought he'd retired to teaching a few years back."

"He's here to prepare you to talk to Kane."

Her eyes widened with surprise. "You set this up?"

"Last night. I know it's hard to believe, but I meant what I said. I aim to keep those promises."

A smile toyed with the corners of her lips. The most beautiful smile he'd ever seen.

He caught himself before he started grinning like an ass. Turning the corner, he gave the conference-room door a rap with his knuckles, pushed it open and focused his attention on Trent Burnell.

Sitting at the conference table amid papers strewn over the desk, Burnell narrowed sharp gray eyes on a small television and DVD player perched high on an AV cart. A recording of Sylvie's visit with Kane from the previous fall flickered on the screen. He glanced up from his scribbled notes and gave the three of them a businesslike nod.

After all Burnell had done in his career, not

only bringing Kane to justice twice, but in the advancement of profiling in the criminal justice system, Reed had expected to be impressed when meeting the man behind the legend. He wasn't disappointed. Although silver was beginning to thread through his dark hair, Burnell looked younger than his years. His sharp features held bright gray eyes that didn't seem to miss a thing. His body held the rock-hard definition that came only with focused exercise. And he exuded the calm authority of a man who'd earned his knowledge through hard work and bad times and had lived to tell the story.

When the interview came to an end, Burnell turned off the DVD player. "Interesting."

Interesting wasn't the term Reed would have chosen. *Bone-chilling* was more like it. Though he'd been in the hospital when Sylvie's visit had taken place, he'd seen the recording. Kane had played the interested listener. Yet under his interest, he'd manipulated Sylvie in her quest for information about Diana's disappearance, eventually steering her to the horrific realization that he was the twins' father.

A fact even Reed hadn't known at that time. And the recognition that the woman he loved, the woman he'd almost married had hidden this truth from him for months still stung like a blistering burn.

Burnell pushed back his chair and rose to his feet. "You must be McCaskey."

Stepping forward, Reed shook Burnell's hand then gestured to the women behind them. "Special Agent Burnell, this is Diana Gale. And Detective Nikki Valducci."

"I'm honored to meet you, sir." Nikki stepped up to shake the FBI profiler's hand with a fan's enthusiasm.

Now *that* was interesting. Nikki had always been ambitious and eager to learn everything she could about the job, but she wasn't exactly the star-struck type.

After exchanging a handshake with Diana, Burnell folded himself back in his chair. The rest of them followed suit, eyeing each other across the conference table.

"My wife, Risa, sends her apologies. She wanted to come, but our son is ill. She decided it was best to stay in D.C."

Diana leaned forward, concern digging a crease between her elegant eyebrows. "I'm sorry to hear that. Will he be okay?"

Burnell waved away Diana's concern. "Just a virus. He'll be fine. But I'm not sorry Risa isn't here. Dryden Kane affected our lives pretty dramatically. I can't pretend this is an easy case for me, or that I'm objective where Kane is concerned. Just so you know."

Tension crept up Reed's spine and settled in his

shoulders. Burnell had faced countless monsters over the years. He'd studied their artwork. He'd crawled inside their minds. If *he* thought Kane wasn't an easy case, what hope did Diana have of facing him down? "Diana is set to visit Kane again this afternoon. We were hoping you could give us some insight about how she should handle him."

"First, there is no handling Kane. Not in the sense of controlling the situation. The man is brilliant. And he's as manipulative as they come. I would guess the chance to dominate and control his adult daughter would be a thrill for him."

Reed leaned forward. Maybe there was a way out of this after all. If Burnell nixed Diana's meeting, Diana would be saved the trauma and emotional pain. At the same time, she couldn't blame Reed for sheltering her. "So what are you saying? That she shouldn't be talking to him?"

He felt her look from across the table.

"It's risky." Burnell focused those sharp eyes on Diana. "I'm not going to pretend it isn't."

"A woman's life is at stake." Diana's voice was as even and determined as her stare.

"You know he'll try to get into your head, manipulate your emotions, use them against you."

"He's already tried."

"He'll succeed."

She shook her head. "It doesn't matter. As long

as I have a chance of learning who the copycat is and where he has taken that woman, it'll be worth it."

Burnell leaned back in his chair and tented his fingers in front of him. "You remind me of Risa."

A smile curved Diana's lips. "I'll take that as a compliment."

"It is. With a good dose of awe mixed in."

Reed leaned back in his chair, tension making the back of his neck throb. So much for any hope of talking Diana out of this crazy plan. Not that he hadn't figured it was a long shot. Now all he could do was make sure she was as prepared as possible. "So what can she do to elicit information, yet still protect herself?"

"The first thing I usually tell an interviewer to do is establish a rapport with the subject. You're way ahead there. He wants to talk. The downside is that he knows a lot about you. Personal things he can use as weapons, to gain your trust, to manipulate your feelings, to hurt you. You have to make sure you don't let him use your emotions against you."

Warnings were all well and good, but Reed was hoping for more specifics. "How can she prevent him from manipulating her emotions?"

"First, don't believe a word he says." Burnell focused on Diana, speaking directly to her. "He'll lie. He'll exaggerate. He'll twist the truth and attack the things dearest to you. Don't take any of it to heart."

"Can I use his emotions against him?"

"Not an easy task. Not with Kane."

"Why not?"

"Men like him don't have feelings for others. Compassion, love, guilt, those things simply don't exist for him."

"So what can I use?"

"With Kane, you have to remember everything is about him. His emotions are about how others make *him* feel and *him* alone. That's what you have to use to get him to open up to you."

"I use how *I* make him feel?"

"Yes."

"How do I know that?"

"When I first arrived this morning, I watched the tapes of your interview with Kane yesterday, and the interview between Kane and your sister from some months ago."

"That's the one you were watching when we came in."

He nodded. "That visit was very interesting. In the conversation with your sister, Kane talked about how he felt after you and Sylvie were born. The way you looked at him made him feel important for the first time in his life. You made him feel like a god, is how he put it. And he implies that made him start feeling dominance in the rest of his life. Dominance over adult women."

Diana leaned forward and splayed her hands on the table. "We were children. He was our father."

"Exactly. It was a natural response on your part." Burnell held up a finger. "But did you hear the defensiveness in your voice just now? You took my statement as a judgment about you, an accusation that you were to blame for him becoming a serial killer. You might recognize rationally that any baby is going to stare adoringly at her parent. But emotionally you responded to the inference that you were the cause of Kane's crimes."

Diana slumped against the back of her chair.

"You can't fall into that trap with Kane. You've got to focus on what he's saying. You can't let yourself simply react emotionally."

She nodded, but this time she looked anything but confident. And Reed had to admit, any confidence he might have conjured up before this meeting was eroding as well.

"Back to his comment about you making him feel like a god."

Diana nodded. "Please."

"Serial killers often struggle with conflicting feelings of inadequacy and superiority. Kane is a perfect example. He craves superiority. He strikes out at people who make him feel inadequate. From

Kane's point of view, you and your sister acknowl-
edged the thing he always wanted to believe about
himself. That he was better than other men. His
mother didn't tell him this. She abused him and
scorned him. His wife didn't tell him this. She
controlled him and had affairs with other men
behind his back. Kane had poor grades in school.
He had acne as a teen. He had trouble holding a
steady job." Burnell glanced down at the papers in
front of him, yet Reed had the impression he knew
most of the facts of Kane's life by heart.

"Then along came his twin girls. Little girls
who adored their daddy and looked up to him.
Little girls who gave him what he saw as his due."

Unease trekked up Reed's spine. "Where are
you leading with this?"

Burnell didn't take his eyes off Diana. "Kane is
going to expect you to look at him the same way
you did as a toddler. More to the point, he is going
to expect you to make him *feel* the same way."

Diana nodded, as if accepting the assignment.

Reed had a little more trouble. "And if she
doesn't?"

"Things can get tricky."

"That's sort of what happened with your wife
Risa, wasn't it? She published an article about him
he didn't like."

Reed had forgotten Nikki was in the room until

she spoke. She leaned forward over the table, just like him and Diana. As if her stake in this case was as personal as theirs.

Burnell paused for a long moment before answering. "She wrote much of the same things I'm telling you right now. She published them in an article for an academic journal. An article Kane didn't appreciate."

Nikki nodded. "And when Kane escaped, he started killing women who looked like her. Then he almost killed Risa herself."

"Among other things." Even though years had passed, tension lined Burnell's face, clenching his jaw. "I've spent my career profiling killers, interviewing them, studying their behavior in order to understand what's important to them, how their minds work, what they might do next. But without a lick of training, Kane figured me inside and out within days. *He* profiled *me*. And it nearly cost Risa her life."

The emotion behind Burnell's words plunged into Reed's chest and twisted like a blade. He turned to Diana, praying to see hesitation in her eyes, second thoughts poised on her tongue.

Eyes on Burnell, she nodded, as if accepting the challenge, as if she were prepared.

Something Reed knew at that moment he would never be.

"Another thing." Burnell pushed a folder across the table to Reed.

Reed flipped open the cover. Inside were the crime-scene reports on the Copycat Killer's third victim—a woman whose body had been so badly burned and mutilated, they were still searching for her identity. He looked up at Burnell, waiting to hear what he had to say.

"Our copycat is deviating from Kane's signature."

Reed nodded. A killer's signature wasn't just about the way he killed or who he chose as a victim, it showed *why* he killed. Kane had used each murder as a type of dress rehearsal, a way to hone his fantasies by killing women who resembled the woman he was obsessed with until he felt ready to go after the woman herself. The copycat had mimicked Kane's signature faithfully with the first two murders. "You mean the copycat is now developing his own signature?"

"It appears so," Burnell said. "He's evolving. Either he was trying to hide this woman's identity, or he is developing his own tastes even as he continues to carry out Kane's orders."

Reed stared at the photo of the body on top of the stack of reports. He didn't know how this situation could get worse, but he had the feeling that was exactly what Burnell was trying to tell him. "What does that mean for us?"

"It means you have two serial killers to worry about."

DIANA LOOKED UP AT THE CAMERA in the corner of the prison interview room. It stared back at her and Kane with its dark eye.

She knew Reed was watching them, listening to every word. But it wasn't enough. She needed to see him. She wanted to look into his warm eyes instead of the impersonal camera lens.

He'd kept his word during the meeting with Trent Burnell. Even though she could tell every impulse in his body was screaming to intervene. Even when she'd walked into this interview room alone to face Kane, he'd merely told her good luck. But in his eyes, she could see how much those two little words had cost him.

"The camera is on."

The low murmur of Kane's voice ripped through her body like an electric charge. She met his emotionless eyes.

"Your boyfriend is watching."

"I don't have a boyfriend."

"Then you shouldn't look at the camera that way or you will."

She sucked in a breath, trying to stem the flow

of blood up her neck and into her cheeks. The last thing she needed was to broadcast to Kane her turmoil. She was supposed to be controlling her emotions and keeping Kane from manipulating her, and already she was off to a bad start. She focused on where the conversation had left off before she'd gotten herself off track with thoughts of Reed. "You didn't answer my question."

"I'm sorry. I was too busy watching you." His smile reached across the distance between their chairs and burrowed under her skin.

She couldn't let him get to her. She had to focus. "I asked how you met this copycat. Have you known him a long time?"

Kane let out a sigh. "I'm here to talk about father-daughter things. Not sit through endless queries from the police."

"When I was here yesterday, you said you would tell me more. About the copycat. About the woman he kidnapped."

"But *you're* not doing the asking. Your mouth might be moving, but Reed McCaskey's questions are coming out."

She didn't like hearing him say Reed's name. She didn't like him thinking about Reed at all. "They're my questions, too."

"You really want to know about this Copycat Killer?"

"Yes."

Kane arched his graying brows. "After what you went through with that professor, I would think hearing the details would be traumatic for you."

And he was right. But she sure as hell wasn't going to admit that to him. "I want to know."

He offered another cold, knowing smile and nothing else.

"You said he was like a son to you," she prompted. "Is he your son?"

"You mean, do you have a brother?"

She leaned forward before she could stop herself. "Do I?"

"Would you like that? To have a brother?"

A brother who was a killer? A brother who was like Dryden Kane? The thought pressed down on her chest like a physical weight. She managed a weak nod.

"Not sure?"

She couldn't lie. "I wouldn't like to have a brother who kills people, no. But I'd like to *know* if I have a brother. Do I?"

"Maybe."

"That's not an answer."

"That's all the answer I'm going to give. At least today."

He was keeping her on the hook, forcing her to

come back. "I'm here now. I don't know if I can make it tomorrow."

"You will. Now tell me about Sylvie's wedding. What kind of music played when she marched down the aisle? Wagner?"

He wanted her to react to the reference to "The Wedding March." Wanted to see how she felt about the music boxes she and Sylvie had received.

She forced herself not to raise her fingers to the heart-shaped pendant Sylvie had given her for being part of her wedding. Instead, she focused on breathing the stale prison air. She couldn't let him see her vulnerability. She couldn't let him get her off track. "Let's say I do have a brother. Does he have the same mother as Sylvie and me?"

"Back to that again."

"Humor me."

"Are you worried that I was—" he hesitated, as if searching for the word "—*screwing* around on your mother?"

Screwing around? Here Kane had brutally murdered close to a dozen people, yet he'd avoided using foul language in front of her? She almost shook her head in disbelief. "Were you?"

He tilted his head to the side, looking at her as if he suspected she was an idiot. "You realize your mother was a whore, don't you?"

She forced herself not to react. "Did you?"

His eyes drove into her, piercing like ice picks. "Not once. Not a single time."

"Then how *might* I have a brother?"

"Your mother wasn't the first."

So it *was* someone in his past. Or at least it might be. She had to remember Kane couldn't be trusted. Any word from his lips could be a lie. But at least Sylvie and Bryce wouldn't be wasting their time in Oshishobee.

"Now you answer a question for me."

The muscles in Diana's back and legs tensed despite her efforts to relax. She didn't want to answer his questions. She didn't want him rummaging around in her mind, trying to control her, manipulate her. But she couldn't very well refuse. She had to give answers in order to get them. "What do you want to know?"

"What do you remember from your childhood?"

"My childhood?"

"Before you were three years old?"

The time when she'd lived with him. The time before he'd murdered her mother. "I don't know. Not much, really."

"Think."

A tremor started deep in her chest. "Just some images, really. Feelings."

"What images? What feelings?" He leaned forward, his handcuffs rattling on the chair arms.

She knew he was looking for something. But what? If she gave the wrong answer, would he get angry? Would he decide he was disappointed in her? That she didn't make him feel as good as she had as a child?

"What do you remember, Diana?"

The tremor moved into her legs, her arms, her hands. She gripped her thighs to stop from shaking. She would have to tell the truth. It was all she had. "I remember playing in a sandbox made from an old tractor tire."

He nodded, urging her to go on.

"I remember a dachshund. It barked a lot. It frightened me."

"It bit you. Do you remember that?"

She searched her mind, but the memory of being bitten wasn't there. "No."

"It was found dead the next day. Slit down the middle and hanging in a tree." His lips pulled back in a smile that left no doubt who had killed it. "What else?"

"I remember a story. Something about a rabbit that ran away. I remember listening to it and feeling very warm. And safe."

His face softened with an eerie look of pleasure. "I read you that story. Every night before I tucked you in bed."

Diana clutched her legs hard and swallowed into

a dry throat. She'd always associated that story with her mother. It couldn't be possible Kane had been the one reading to her. It couldn't be possible *he* was responsible for those warm, safe feelings. The most normal feelings she'd experienced as a child.

"What's wrong, Diana?"

Trent Burnell's warnings rang in her ears. Kane could be lying. He could be using her childhood emotions to manipulate her. She had to regain control of herself. "Nothing's wrong."

"You don't believe that you could have loved a serial killer? You don't believe I could have been a good father?"

She didn't. She couldn't. The thought was abhorrent. He had to be lying, manipulating her. She had to hold on to that.

She thought of what Kane had told Sylvie—of how she and her sister had made him feel. If he was using the only good feelings about her childhood to manipulate her, maybe she could return the favor. Maybe she could manipulate Kane right back. "I do remember the feelings I had as a child. Good feelings."

"I bought you presents. Little dresses. Music boxes. I did all the things a good father does."

She forced herself to nod.

"You and Sylvie adored me. When you saw me, you would smile so hard your faces would glow.

You would ask for me to give you your bath. You would sit on my lap when we watched TV."

"I remember."

He arched a brow. "Do you?"

"To us, you were the most important man in the world. We worshipped you."

His smile faded. His expression grew as cold as his eyes. "You don't remember, do you?"

"Yes, I do. I remember the feelings. The impressions."

"Who told you to say that?"

Her stomach seized. She wiped her palms on her jeans and gripped her thighs harder. "No one told me to say anything. What do you mean?"

"The part about how I was the most important man in the world. That you worshipped me. Someone told you to play up to me. Who was it?"

Oh, God, she shouldn't have pushed it. She should have stuck to the truth and kept her mouth shut otherwise. Hadn't Trent warned her about how intelligent Kane was? How well he could read people? Hadn't she already witnessed that herself?

"Were you talking to the FBI, Diana?"

Her blood froze in her veins.

"Who did they send? A profiler? Did he tell you what I dream about at night? Did he tell you what *makes me tick?*" He fired the words at her, staccato as bullets.

Diana forced herself to remain in her chair. She forced herself to meet his eyes. "I remembered the story about the rabbit. I remembered the feelings."

"But you don't remember the profiler's name?"

She dropped her gaze to the floor.

"Was it Trent Burnell?" Kane's voice was quiet and thick with hate.

She tried to focus. She tried not to react.

"I see how it is. It isn't just McCaskey's words you're reciting. Burnell has made you into his puppet. Just like the puppet you played with as a child. The puppet I bought for you." He jerked up on his arms. The cuffs clanged against the chair.

Diana flinched. She half expected him to break free, to reach out and grab her by the throat.

"No daughter of mine is going to be Burnell's puppet. You wanted to know who the copycat is? You wanted to know where he took that woman? You'll have to ask Burnell."

She shook her head, her hair whipping her cheeks. "It's not like that. I only talked to him for a few minutes. He's not even here anymore. He left this morning."

"Then you're out of luck."

And so was Nadine Washburn. "No, please. Listen to me."

"I did. I didn't like what I heard." His lips pulled back in a cross between a smile and a snarl. "There was one part of being a father I didn't like. Playing the disciplinarian. But sometimes it has to be done."

"What are you saying?"

"That sometimes children need to be taught a lesson."

"A lesson?" Her head whirled. She could only imagine what kind of cruel lesson he would teach. The tremble enveloped her, closing over her head like water. Drowning her.

"Learn it well, Diana. And the next time you come to see me, you'd better be on your knees."

Chapter Nine

Head pounding with Kane's quiet words, Reed followed Corrections Officer Nathan Seides's broad shoulders out of the prison in silence, Diana by his side. It wasn't until after he'd signed out, retrieved his pistol and settled into the driver's seat of his sedan that he was able to convince his voice to function.

"I'm so sorry, Diana. I never should have asked Burnell to come. I should have known Kane would sense you'd talked to someone."

Diana fastened her seat belt with shaking hands. Folding her arms across her chest, she stared through the bug-spattered windshield. "I was the one who blew it."

"You? You were great in there."

"No, I wasn't. I tried too hard. I told him I remembered things I didn't. I knew I had to be honest with him or he'd know I was lying. But I wasn't." She shook her head. "I only knew a few warm, safe feelings in my childhood. One was that story. That feeling I had when it was read to me. I just couldn't stand the thought that *he* was responsible for that. Do you think he was?"

He knew what she wanted to hear. And he wanted with all his heart to pronounce Kane a liar. But he'd promised last night he would give things to her straight. "I don't know."

"I guess it doesn't matter. We can't change what happened. But I'm afraid for Nadine, Reed. I'm afraid the copycat is going to kill her because of me."

Reed wanted to reassure her, tell her they would find Nadine Washburn, that she would be okay. But he couldn't do that. No more than he could make pronouncements he didn't know to be true. "His intention was to kill her all along, Diana. Remember that."

She opened her mouth to protest.

He held up a hand. "Serial killers don't just kidnap, they kill. Our chances of finding Nadine alive might be slimmer after this, but they were almost nonexistent from the beginning."

He knew she didn't want to believe it. Hell, he didn't blame her. Even with all she'd been through in her twenty-three years, she hadn't seen even a small fraction of life's underbelly. He hoped she never had to experience more of it than she already had. "We need to be more covert about your involvement in the case. For your safety. There's no point in egging Kane on."

"Covert? What does that mean? That I sit in my hotel room and knit?"

And you don't come out until this is over. He took a deep breath, trying to come up with a more tactful way of saying it. "Being seen riding around with me isn't a good idea."

"But I can go to the district office, right? I can help there."

He shifted in his seat, trying to stave off the pain from another shot of acid to his burgeoning ulcer.

"As long as I don't *go* anywhere, Kane won't know the difference, right?"

"I suppose you're right. And we could use your help. The paperwork that goes with coordinating a case like this is staggering. We never have enough civilian support staff." Of course, with all Diana knew about Kane, she brought more to the table than the average civilian. And she'd certainly be safe sitting in the district office surrounded by police. The wheels in his mind started turning, thinking of ways she might be able to help.

He started the car, the AC slapping him in the face with a bout of refreshingly cold air. He had to admit, he was more comfortable with the thought of Diana being where he could see her, watch over her. He wasn't dumb enough to tell her that after their discussion last night, but he liked the idea all the same.

Even though every hour with her made it harder and harder to remember she was no longer his.

He focused on the case, turning things over in his mind as they made the hour drive back to Madison.

They reached the shadow of the state capitol at about one o'clock and circled on the one-way street a block off the capitol square. Turning on Carroll Street, they approached the district office entrance.

A crowd had gathered on the sidewalk. As television cameras turned to capture his and Diana's images, ice descended into his gut. "Damn Perreth. He must have convinced the lieutenant to issue a press release. Or he just booked it. I'm going to choke the living—" He hit the gas, cruising right past the swarm of reporters and cameras. He turned right onto another one-way street and started winding his way around the block. "We'll go in through the garage. Hopefully the buzzards don't have that door staked out."

"So much for Kane not seeing us together."

"They haven't gotten a clear shot yet." He turned back onto Doty Street. If he was smart, he'd take Diana straight to the hotel, no matter what her protests.

He glanced at her. Despite the determined set to

her chin, fine lines rimmed her lips and dug between her eyebrows.

What he wouldn't give to smooth those lines away with his fingers. What he wouldn't give to hit the highway and keep driving until she was far away from Dryden Kane.

Maybe she was right. Maybe he would always try to take care of her, despite the odds, despite his failures. Maybe he would never change. Maybe, if he was honest with himself, he didn't even want to.

A weight settled in his chest, making it difficult to breathe. He swung onto Martin Luther King Jr. Boulevard, passing the main entrance to the City County Building. A smattering of people stood at the entrance, waiting to pass through the metal detectors. Jurors and office personnel returning from lunch? Or reporters? He couldn't tell. Taking the next turn onto Wilson Street, he braced himself.

The block was nearly vacant except for a single man standing near the door to the police garage. "I should have known."

"Who is he?"

"Aidan Powell. Reporter for the *Capital Times*. A real pain in the ass. The good thing is, I think we can avoid photos and names." He swung the car to the curb. Hitting the button to open the garage door, he lowered his window. "I should have known you'd be here."

"Got a chance to talk, Detective?" Powell ducked his head, trying to get a look inside the car.

"I'll have to get back to you, but I'm sure we can work something out."

"You know I'll hold you to that."

"I know." Reed hit the gas, breathing a sigh of relief. "Powell's a good guy, for a reporter."

"So you're going to talk to him?"

Reed nodded. "I'll talk. Perreth's right about one thing. The press can be very helpful in cases like this…when they aren't plastering every leaked word all over the news." He could only hope Perreth hadn't mentioned that Dryden Kane's daughters were helping on the case. That would produce the kind of copy that would turn even ethical reporters like Aidan Powell into rabid dogs.

Closing the garage door securely behind them, Reed piloted the car into his assigned spot. So far, so good. He got out and led Diana through the garage and into the adjoining offices. The place still smelled like a sewer. Hopefully the lieutenant had procured some office space for the task force. Not only would he have a blistering headache if he had to breathe this smell all day and night, with both the central and east districts operating out of this building, they would never have enough space for the task force now that it would be going full tilt again.

Reed glanced out the station's front door. Ellen Yee sat at the reception desk, the gate before the flood of reporters outside. Ellen had a ways to grow to hit the five-foot mark and had only been with the department a year, but she was tougher than any street punk. As long as the national media hadn't descended, she would keep the reporters in line. Reed suspected the locals were a little bit afraid of her.

Too bad Ellen couldn't keep Stan Perreth out.

The moment Reed spotted him, it was all he could do to keep from slamming his fist into that bulldog face.

The detective flipped an unlit cigarette in stained fingers and glared at Diana. "Is bringing your girlfriend to work going to be an everyday thing now, McCaskey?"

Reed didn't bother answering. Instead, he turned to Diana. He didn't like Perreth's comments about her, but he liked the way the bastard looked at her even less. "I'll meet you in the conference room." He held his breath, praying she wouldn't argue and make this a bigger mess than it was already.

To his relief, she nodded and peeled off down the side hall.

Reed jabbed the videotape from the prison at Perreth. "Make copies of this. VHS and DVD."

"I'm not your errand boy."

"Actually, if you want to stay on this task force, you are."

"I don't have time. I'm getting ready to give a statement to the press."

"I haven't approved a statement. In fact, I told you we were going to wait on informing the media."

"I don't need your approval. I have the lieutenant's."

"And he told you to run it by me then, I'm sure." Reed grabbed the paper out of Perreth's hand, causing him to drop the cigarette. As Perreth stooped to pick it up, Reed skimmed the statement.

Just as he'd feared, Perreth had sprinkled Diana's name throughout his statement, even going so far as to identify her as Dryden Kane's daughter.

Reed crumpled it with one hand. "You're not mentioning Diana's role in this. And you're *not* admitting she's here."

"Why the hell not? She doesn't get special protection just because you're—"

"It's not special protection. Copy the tape, and while you're at it, watch the damn thing. Then you'll understand why we need to keep her presence here quiet." He thrust the tape into Perreth's hand.

He stepped away from Perreth before he gave into his urges and slugged the guy, and joined Diana and Nikki in the conference room. "Any word on office space that doesn't reek?"

Nikki raised a brow. "No word yet. But count yourselves lucky. Except for my little vacation to the north district this morning, I've been steeping in it like a tea bag for twenty-four hours."

Voices erupted from outside the conference room. Diana and Nikki looked up at Reed. He held up a hand. "I'll see what it's about."

He'd just turned around when all five-foot-eleven of Meredith Unger burst through the door.

Ellen Yee chased in her wake. "You can't just barge in there—"

"We need to talk, McCaskey."

He couldn't agree more. "I've got it, Ellen."

"Thanks." Spinning around, the petite woman rushed back to her post to block any reporters who might try to run the play Meredith Unger just had.

Reed glared at the attorney. Meredith Unger had the rep of a shark and the size of a small football player. Although she didn't work criminal cases much anymore, Reed had sat in the hot seat during a few of her cross-examinations in the past. Even then he'd never known her to be this zealous. "What's going on?"

She flipped a hank of platinum hair back over her shoulder. "Who the hell gave you permission to talk to my client without me present?"

"Your client?"

"Don't play dumb."

"Who's playing?" Here he'd thought yesterday was a bad day. This day was shaping up to be straight out of hell. Reed's gaze shot to Diana. A reflex. And a bad one.

"This is her, isn't it? The daughter?" Meredith raised a plucked brow. "I knew it."

Reed shook his head. He couldn't believe this. For someone who was trying to keep Diana's presence here from Dryden Kane, he was doing a damned awful job. "What is it you think you know?"

"Her presence here says everything. This woman isn't visiting my client because she's his long-lost family. She's manipulating him. She's working as an agent of the police."

DIANA FOLDED HER ARMS around her middle and hunched forward in the conference-room chair. Her head spun, making her feel as dizzy and queasy as if she were on a carnival ride. She hadn't stopped shaking since her visit to Kane. And with the press and Perreth and Meredith Unger swirling around her ever since, she felt thoroughly disoriented. And now Kane's attorney thought *she* was manipulating *him?*

The irony was as thick as the scent of sewer.

She had told Reed she wanted to stand alone. That she wanted to take care of herself. And she did. But she couldn't help being grateful he was with her. She didn't know how she would have survived this morning without him.

He had successfully sequestered Meredith Unger in his office with Nikki, promising to join them directly. Now he stood at the other end of the room barking orders to Perreth. "Search court records. I want to see a client list for Meredith Unger."

"Do you really think she's Kane's connection to the copycat? Or are you just looking to waste my time?"

"Why? You have somewhere else to be?"

Perreth tapped a cigarette from his pack and glanced longingly out the door.

"I didn't think so."

Heaving a theatrical sigh, Perreth ambled out of the conference room, walking past Diana as if she weren't there.

Another thing to be grateful for.

Diana watched him go, glad to have a moment alone with Reed. She should probably tell him he was right, that she should have stayed away from the district office, that she should have holed up in her hotel room. But the thought of sitting helpless in her room was worse than any amount of dirty looks Perreth could throw at her, or inferences Meredith Unger could make. "What is Meredith Unger going to do?"

"Do? Beyond making our lives hell?" He

rubbed a hand over his face. "I suppose she's getting ready to argue that any action Kane takes after his talks with you was set up by police. Entrapment, or some kind of garbage."

"And she can get away with that?"

"I didn't say that. Just that she'll try. The worst thing about her barging in here is that I can almost guarantee she'll tell Kane you were here."

Great. But he didn't have to tell her that. "So what do we do now?"

Reed grabbed a pile of papers Nikki had left on the conference table. He plopped them on the table in front of Diana. "Since you're here, you might as well get some work done. Besides, no matter what Meredith Unger passes on to Kane, this is still probably the safest place for you."

Diana picked the top form off the stack. "Missing persons reports?"

"These are from last September and October from all over the country—or at least from those jurisdictions that have computerized their reports. We've already done a computer search to come up with women who match the characteristics of our victim."

"The body that was burned?" Diana shuddered. The body who was at first mistaken for her.

"Burnell said the copycat burned the body either to act out his own fantasies or to hide her identity. If we can figure out who she was, we'll be that much closer to finding our copycat." He tapped a finger on the top of the pile. "Right now, we're at a dead end. I'm hoping with what you know about Kane, you might be able to recognize something in these reports that can help kick-start our investigation."

She nodded. She could do that. She was eager to do that. "And what are you going to do?"

"I'm going to try to appeal to the human side of Meredith Unger. Provided there is one." He leaned over her and brushed his lips to her forehead. "I'll be back for you."

As soon as he stepped out the door, she leaned back in her chair, heart slamming against her rib cage as if she'd just finished a ten-mile run. She raised her hand to her forehead, touching her fingertips to the spot he'd kissed. As sweet as the gesture had been, she couldn't help thinking how she wished he hadn't done it.

How she wished he'd kissed her lips instead.

She shook her head and riveted her attention to the papers in front of her. The stack rose several inches thick. So many women. How many of them were the victims of violent death? Picking the top report from the stack, she forced her mind to concentrate on the information it contained.

She scanned the missing person's description and moved down the page. Moving her eyes over license plate and vehicle information, she studied the section marked Other Information, a classification including the complainant, the reporting officer and the clothing and jewelry the woman had worn when she'd disappeared. "Diana?"

She didn't recognize the thin voice at first. It was so out of context. She turned around.

Louis Ingersoll leaned against the doorjamb. "Hey."

"Louis? What are you doing here?"

He didn't meet her gaze; instead, he focused on her neck. "I suppose *he* gave that to you."

Her hand flew to her throat. She clutched the delicate heart necklace in her fingers. The necklace she wore to feel close to her sister. "It's from Sylvie." She didn't know why she felt she had to explain. She'd told Louis she wasn't comfortable with his gift. She'd told him she liked him as a friend and that she couldn't be anything more. But the hurt and anger in his eyes when he saw she wasn't wearing the necklace he'd given her, but another, made her feel she had to give him an explanation just the same.

He narrowed his eyes. "For the wedding?"

"What?"

"Did she give you that for being in her wedding?"

"Yes. It was my maid-of-honor gift."

His face relaxed into the Louis she knew.

She glanced at the conference room. The last

thing she needed was for Reed to walk in about now. This day had been disturbing enough without trying to referee a face-off between the two. "Why are you here?"

He shook his head, as if he wasn't sure. "Something happened at our building yesterday, I guess. The police asked me to come down. Is that why you're here?" He eyed the stack of paper in front of her.

"Not totally." She hated lying to Louis, but she was sure Reed wouldn't want her to tell Louis anything. Still, it didn't feel right to avoid answering his simple question. "I'm going through some paperwork."

"You're working for the police?" His eyes widened, then narrowed. "Or for McCaskey?"

The jealousy again. She didn't know if they'd ever get around that, if they'd ever be friends again. "I can't tell you any more than that. I'm sorry."

His face flushed red, blending skin and freckles and hair.

She felt bad for Louis, but what could she do to satisfy him, short of falling madly in love with him? Something that just plain was not going to happen. "I'm not back together with Reed." She flinched. There she was, explaining things again.

"That's not what it looks like."

"I don't want to talk about this."

"You used to talk to me, Diana. We talked all the time. What happened?"

What happened? How was she supposed to answer that? Louis's feelings happened. He started looking at her as if he had a claim. He started acting as if he deserved an explanation for every decision she made. He started giving her gifts.

"Someone left a music box outside my apartment door yesterday. Did you see anyone unfamiliar in the building?"

His rigid posture seem to relax a little. "No."

Maybe if she could steer their conversation off the subject of Reed, they could stay clear of hurt feelings. "That's probably what the police want to talk to you about."

He took a step into the room. "That's not what the detective said."

"What did he say?"

"I'm only supposed to talk to him. No other detective. No one else."

Odd. Why would a detective give Louis those kinds of instructions? "Who was the detective?"

"His name is Perreth."

A bad feeling solidified in the pit of her stomach. Why would Perreth tell Louis not to talk to another detective? What was he up to? "Louis, you have to tell me what Perreth said."

He shook his head, the fluorescent light flaming orange off his hair. "I can't."

"Please. It might be important."

"Sorry, Diana. I know who you're going to run to as soon as I tell you anything. And Detective Perreth specifically said not to say a word to McCaskey."

"SO WHAT DO YOU THINK he's up to?" Diana had been mulling over what Louis had told her about Perreth all afternoon and evening while she'd sorted through missing persons reports. She hadn't come up with an explanation that made sense, but her uneasy feeling about the whole exchange had grown.

Alternating shadow and streetlight played across Reed's face as they drove the few blocks to her hotel. "What Perreth's up to is *always* the question. And I don't have the answer this time."

"Do you think he's doing something to hurt you?" Ever since Reed had confronted Perreth about abusing his wife, the bulldog-faced detective had been looking for revenge.

"I can almost guarantee he is trying to hurt me. He's probably trying to get me thrown off the task force. And if he can, ruin my career."

"How would he do that?"

"If I knew that, I could head him off." He flicked on his signal and made a turn, circling toward the hotel. "Perreth is no genius, but he can be creative.

At least when he's properly motivated. And I guess we don't have to wonder if Louis Ingersoll would be eager to help."

Diana didn't have to spend much time thinking to answer that one. "If Perreth's plan is to hurt you, Louis would help in a heartbeat."

"I know he's your friend. What I don't understand is why."

Things might have changed between her and Louis in past months, but it hadn't changed so much that she didn't remember exactly why she'd valued his friendship. "He didn't judge me."

Reed's brows snapped upward. "And I did?"

"No. Not really. But I felt like I was letting you down just the same."

"Letting me down? How? You never let me down."

She shook her head. He was right. She could see that now. Reed had thrived on helping her, taking care of her. The only person she had let down was herself. "I suppose my failings were mostly in my own head. But at the time, Louis seemed safe. It really never occurred to me that he wanted more than friendship. Not until after you and I broke up."

"What happened?"

"He started coming over to my apartment more. He'd stop to see me at the university every time the food-service company he works for had a delivery downtown. And he gave me an expensive necklace for a Christmas present. Emeralds and diamonds set in white gold."

"Nice." His gaze flicked to her throat, as if checking to see what jewelry she was wearing.

"I never wore it. I knew he would take it as a sign that I wanted to be romantically involved, which I didn't."

"You gave it back?"

She shifted in her seat. "Well, no."

"Why not?"

She stared out the side window at the night street scrolling by. She knew she should have insisted Louis take back the gift. But somehow, she couldn't. "He just felt so fragile. So needy. If I had, I would have broken his heart. I didn't know what to do. So I put it in my drawer and forgot about it." At least she'd tried. With Louis checking her throat nearly every time she saw him, she hadn't been able to wipe it from her mind for good.

"He clearly sees me as his rival."

She couldn't argue with that. And the way it looked, Louis was now conspiring with Perreth to sabotage Reed's career. "I'll talk to him. I'll tell him to leave you out of this."

"And you think that will help?"

"Probably not. But if there's a danger to your career, I can't just do nothing." Reed's career was more important to him than anything. She couldn't live with herself if her actions ended up destroying it.

He veered the car into a vacant spot along the curb, parking between a van and a cab dropping off its fare. Slipping the key from the ignition, he twisted to face her, his hand braced against the back of her seat. "Everything will be fine."

God help her, she wanted to believe him. She wanted to grab onto his words and hold them close to her heart. But she knew it wasn't that easy. Things were never that easy. "You promised to be straight with me, not to smooth things over."

"Okay then, it might not be fine. But whatever happens, we'll deal with it. Better?" Giving her arm a light pat, he spun around and climbed from the car.

Better? Hardly. But at least her eyes were wide open. At least she was seeing everything in front of her, facing everything she needed to face.

She retrieved a file of missing-person reports Reed had allowed her to take from the district office and climbed out of the car. They crossed the lobby and caught an elevator. Once inside, Diana leaned against the mirrored wall, fatigue descending into her body and hissing through her mind.

It would feel good to be alone for a few hours. Quiet. Safe. After suffering through the jangle of activity at the district office for hour upon hour,

Diana could hardly think. She had no idea how Reed could force himself to go back there and work through the night, but she had no doubt that was his plan.

Nadine was still out there, and time was ticking away.

The elevator opened and she followed Reed into the vacant hall.

"Damn." Reed checked his watch. "It's after midnight. There should be an officer waiting here."

"He's only a little late." She probably should have stayed at the City County Building after all. Reed couldn't afford to waste his precious time babysitting her. He needed to get back to work. He needed to find Nadine. "I can stay alone for a little while. It isn't as if the door doesn't lock."

"You're not staying alone." He flipped open his phone and punched in a number.

Diana tamped down a spike of frustration. Reed had lived up to their bargain today. He hadn't hovered. He'd let her help with the case. He'd even been straight with her when she'd prodded. She hadn't believed he'd be able to keep up his end, but he had for the most part. If he insisted an officer stay outside her door, she could go along with that. If she were honest with herself, after Kane's harsh words about discipline this morning, she didn't exactly want to be alone.

She fished her key card from her purse and swiped it through the lock. Light flashing green, she turned the door's handle. "We might as well wait inside." She pushed the door open.

The sickly sweet smell of death and decay hit her like a blanket. Choking her. Gagging her. Bringing her to her knees.

Chapter Ten

Reed grasped Diana's arm, holding her, keeping her on her feet. He didn't have to check the body to see if she was still alive. Splayed naked on the bedspread, Nadine Washburn was killed in the same manner as Kane and the copycat's previous victims. Blond hair streaked with blood tangled around a pale face and dull eyes stared up at the ceiling, frozen in horror.

Anger worked up Reed's throat, as bitter as bile.

He scanned the flowered spread, the carpet, the furniture, making quick mental notes of each smudge of blood or piece of lint that might be out of place.

"My punishment," Diana said, her voice barely a whisper. She clutched the file of missing persons forms to her chest, hugging it like a doll.

Reed slipped his arm more securely around her and pulled her trembling body tight to his side. He wanted to whisk her away, convince her this had nothing to do with her, convince himself. But obviously that would be impossible.

Out in the hall, the elevator swooshed open. Reed released Diana, turning in time to see Officer Drummond tromping down the hall.

He joined them in the doorway. "Sorry I'm late, Detective. I got hung up on State Street. I had to babysit a drunk frat kid puking in the gutter. Real nice. I bet his parents would be proud." He glanced past them and into the room. His mouth dropped open. "Holy cow."

Reed released Diana. Once he was certain she could stand under her own power, he turned to give the young officer a glare. He would address his tardiness later. Right now he needed the kid to focus strictly on the job. "I want you to call it in, then set up an outer perimeter. No one leaves this hotel without being interviewed, especially all employees. And I want this floor, the laundry, the kitchen and anywhere else he might have gained access to the hotel and the key to this room sealed. And I need a master key to the rooms on this floor."

Drummond nodded his cropped head. He backed from the room. "Will do."

"And Drummond?"

"Yeah?"

"This is the Copycat Killer's work. Speed is of the essence. We can't afford any mistakes."

"Sure thing." He gave a military nod. Spinning on a heel, the young cop raced for the elevator.

Reed turned back to Diana. She'd inched farther into the room while he'd been talking to Drummond. Eyes glazed and sunken, she stared at the body as if in a trance.

He'd seen that vacant look in victims' eyes before. The look of shock. Of course, in the past two days, Diana hadn't merely suffered one shock, she'd suffered many. He could only hope that after all she'd been through, her body didn't pick this moment to allow the stress to come crashing down on her. "Come on, Di. I need to get you out of here." He slipped an arm around her shoulder and guided her away from the body and toward the hall.

Suddenly she stopped, grasping the doorjamb as if desperate to prevent him from ushering her from the room. "No, wait…"

"You can't do anything here, Diana."

"I know. I just…"

She wasn't thinking. She probably wasn't even feeling. She was just resisting his arm around her. Resisting his concern. Resisting *him*.

He shook off the sting. It didn't matter. Not now. He needed to make sure she was okay. As okay as she possibly could be. And letting her stare at Nadine Washburn's body even another second wouldn't help. "This is a crime scene. I need to preserve whatever he might have left behind. I can't have you contaminating possible evidence."

She released the door frame and held her hand to her forehead. "I never thought of that. I'm sorry."

"You're in shock. Disoriented. It's okay." He guided her into the hall.

She shook her head. "It's not okay, Reed. He said he would discipline me. He said the next time he saw me, he wanted me on my knees. I should have seen something like this coming. I kind of felt it, but—"

"There was nothing you could have done."

She looked up at him, desperation gleaming in her eyes. "She died because of me."

"No, she didn't." At least he could relieve that burden from her shoulders.

"She did. He said he would punish me for talking to Trent Burnell. He killed her to punish me."

"I don't care what he said. She didn't die because of what happened in your visit with Kane."

"How do you know?"

"Did you notice how her body was lying flat to the bed? The way her muscles looked relaxed, as if she was asleep?"

"Yeah…"

"A body's muscles start to become rigid a couple hours after death."

She nodded, as if she was following, understanding. "Rigor mortis."

"Right." He let out a relieved breath. She was following. Thinking. Maybe the shock wasn't too much for her. Maybe she would be okay. "I can't be certain, not until the body's examined. But it looks to me as if the rigor is already relaxing. And judging by the smell, she didn't die within the last two hours."

"So when did she die?"

"I can't say for sure, but depending on conditions, I'd guess her time of death to be sometime last night."

"That means she was already dead. When Kane said those things, she'd been dead for hours."

"I'm guessing your punishment was finding her in your bed. Unless he planned that all along, too."

She still looked pale, her eyes troubled. But there was a strength in the way she held her spine he'd never noticed before. Upright. Straight. As if she was preparing herself to meet head-on whatever might hit her next. She met his eyes and nodded. "Thanks."

"For what?"

"Just being honest with me, explaining things. Instead of trying to sweep me away and fix everything."

He swallowed hard, his throat aching all the way down to his gut. He'd wanted to do exactly what she'd said. He'd wanted to shelter her, take care of her. He'd been trying to do just that when she'd grabbed the edge of the door, when she'd prevented him from whisking her from the room. He felt like a fraud accepting credit he didn't deserve.

But he nodded anyway.

Taking a deep breath to clear his mind, he gestured to a small seating area halfway down the hall. "Why don't you wait down there? When Drummond sends up the master key, I'll open a room for you. You can lie down, get some rest."

She nodded. "Right. You have a job to do."

Yes, a job. He thought of Nadine Washburn's mutilated body and the shadow of a wavy-soled footprint he thought he'd spotted on the carpet near the bed. It would be another long night.

She'd just taken a step when the bleat of a cell phone cut the air.

Reed pushed his suit coat to the side and glanced at the phone on his belt. "Not mine."

Diana balanced the thick file in one arm while she fished her phone from her purse. Flipping it open, she held it to her ear, her hand visibly shaky. "Hello?" Her eyes grew wide and shot to Reed's face.

Another shot of adrenaline slammed into his bloodstream. "What is it?"

"Are you sure?" What little blood still colored Diana's cheeks drained. "Okay. I'll let you talk to Reed."

She pulled the phone from her ear and held

it out to him. "It's Sylvie. She and Bryce are on their way back."

"On their way back?"

"They've found our brother. And he lives in the Madison area."

He took the phone from her hand. The current location of Diana's half brother wasn't wasted on him. And judging from the tone of her voice, it wasn't wasted on Diana either. The killer who had struck tonight, the man revisiting Kane's sick fantasies, might be Diana's own blood.

The son of Dryden Kane.

Chapter Eleven

He watched the single light in the window of the gargantuan stone mansion on the edge of Lake Mendota. The husband was gone, at least overnight. He was sure of it. He'd watched him pack his bags in his car this afternoon. The wife would be alone. At least she would be until tonight. When she stepped outside on her terrace for her nightly glass of chardonnay, he'd be there.

He checked his syringe, his bag, the gardener's cart in the back of his van. With the thick trees hugging the lot's perimeter, this would be a piece of cake. Even easier than the Laundromat.

And as soon as he bagged this one for Dryden Kane, he'd figure out how to get his hands on what he really wanted.

Diana Gale.

He tightened at the thought of her. She might

think she was superior to him now, so superior she couldn't even see him, but she'd change that tune.

He slipped a hand into his bag and pulled out the pink lace bra and matching panties he'd taken from Diana's suitcase in the hotel.

It wouldn't be long now. He'd grab this one tonight, and then look for a way to get his hands on what he really wanted. He'd pretend Dryden Kane had given her to him. Handed her over as the father gives the bride. Then he'd take her for a ride she'd never forget. Not a ride that would end in a few days with hunting and gutting a carcass. But a ride that would stretch in front of them like a never-ending honeymoon.

She would belong to him.

At the mansion, the porch light switched on and a slender, dark-haired woman stepped onto the patio, her wineglass shining clear and light yellow in her hand. A breeze kicked up from the west, lifting her hair and the hem of her skirt. Beautiful. Vulnerable. But he didn't feel the surge of pleasure warm his blood for her. Not as he did just thinking of Diana down on the floor, doing his bidding.

He turned off the dome light in his van and opened the door. Grabbing his bag and syringe, he slipped out and circled to the back to fetch the other tools of his trade.

He'd do his job tonight. Take this one to the place he'd taken the others. Tie her tight and secure. Wait for Kane's further instructions.

And then he'd focus on Diana Gale.

Chapter Twelve

"His name is Cordell Turner."

Diana leaned back in her chair next to Sylvie, Bryce and Nikki in the task force's new odor-free digs as Reed explained what Bryce and Sylvie had discovered in Oshishobee. Eyes red and chin dark with stubble, Diana was sure he hadn't slept all night. Not that she had fared much better.

She'd spent the night huddling in a hotel room, listening to the murmur of the officers' voices in the hall outside. Every time she'd tried to sleep, she'd seen Nadine Washburn's mutilated body. Every time she'd tried to dream, her mind had bombarded her with questions about Dryden Kane's son—her and Sylvie's half brother. Was he trying to walk in his father's footsteps? Was he following the family legacy?

The thought made her feel sick.

She glanced at her sister. Sylvie gripped the

edge of the conference table, as if she were barely holding on. Diana could only imagine how hard this new revelation was on her. Especially now, when she needed all her strength to cope with the changes her body was going through.

Reed looked her in the eye before continuing. "And he has a criminal record."

Diana leaned forward in her chair. The back of her neck prickled. Apparently her fears of a family legacy weren't that far off. "What did he do?"

"Killed a man when he was eighteen. He did eight years for manslaughter."

"My God." Diana's mind spun. She'd never had any idealistic illusions about family, not like Sylvie had. After all, she'd grown up under Ed Gale's cruel thumb. But this? A father who was a serial killer? A brother who, at the very least, had murdered one man?

Nikki looked down at the notebook in her hands. "He made parole two years ago and has been clean since."

"As far as we know," added Reed. "He lives in an apartment on the west side. Washes windows. His own business. Somehow he convinces people to let him into their homes."

"Sounds like a good opportunity to find potential victims," Bryce said.

Diana had to agree. There were many ways he

could have used his access to women's homes and businesses to stalk them. Even his first two victims, college coeds like the women Dryden Kane had killed, could have come to his attention while he'd been doing his job. Diana suppressed a shudder. She doubted she would ever be able to let any stranger into her home after this. Not without planning how to defend herself. "So what happens now?"

"We have a word with him," Reed said.

"We?"

"Nikki and me. But if you want to ride along, you can take a look. See if you recognize him."

"You think I might have seen him before?"

He shrugged. "Maybe in your building. Or at the university. If Turner is the copycat, I can almost guarantee he's been keeping an eye on you for Kane. Probably for quite a while. Are you up to it?"

Diana had wanted Reed to have faith in her, to let her help with the case. The fact that he was, even after the trauma of finding the body in her bed last night, wasn't lost on her. "Of course I'm up to it."

"Good." He gave her an understanding smile, as if he recognized the doubts and questions swirling in her mind about her brother. "What is it?"

She shook her head. She wasn't sure. Maybe a feeling. Maybe just doubt. "You really think Cordell Turner could be the copycat?"

"I don't know. But if he is, I'm going to get

him. Whether he's your brother or not, he needs to be stopped."

She nodded. Of course, that went without saying. "That's not what's bothering me."

"Then what is?"

"Kane." She could feel Sylvie, Bryce and Nikki watching her, but she kept her focus on Reed. "I have to think he made that 'like a son' comment purposely to lead us to Cordell Turner. But if Turner is the copycat, why would Kane want to point us in his direction?"

"Maybe it was a mistake, a slip he didn't intend to make," Sylvie said.

Diana shook her head. "I don't think Kane makes slips he doesn't intend. I think every word from his lips is thought out, calculated."

Reed nodded thoughtfully.

"He told me about Sylvie when I visited him last year because he knew I would try to find her. He wanted to draw her in. Get her to visit the prison. He was frustrated when I didn't tell her about him."

"So you think he might be using the same tactic to establish contact with his son?"

"It seems like something he might do."

Reed nodded. "It sounds plausible. If he doesn't have contact already. If Turner is not the copycat."

Her chest ached, as if the pressure outside her

body was too much to stand against. The idea that their brother had followed in Kane's murdering footsteps weighed on her.

Reed leaned across the table, focusing on her as if they were the only two in the room. "Trust the evidence, Diana. Information in a police investigation is not a science. At best, it's an art form. At worst, just a confusing mess. Hard physical evidence is the only thing that can't be faked or nuanced or spun. In the long run, it's the only thing that tells the real story."

Diana grabbed on to his words. He was right. She didn't have to guess about her brother, and neither did the police. If hard evidence proved Cord Turner was the Copycat Killer, then he would go back to prison. And if he was a pawn being moved around the board by Kane, the evidence would show that, too. "When do we leave?"

"As soon as possible." Reed gave her a tight-lipped smile and turned to her sister. "Sylvie? Do you want to come, too?"

Diana braced herself, trying to beat back her concern. She didn't want Sylvie anywhere near Cordell Turner any more than she wanted her visiting Dryden Kane. Whether her brother was the Copycat Killer or not, he was still a murderer. And their meeting would likely be traumatic no matter what kind of truth came out.

Sylvie swallowed hard. She gripped the table harder, her knuckles blanching. "You'd better count me out."

"You sure?"

"Yeah."

Diana couldn't help be relieved. As relieved as worry for her sister would allow. If Sylvie was bowing out, she must really be sick. "Are you okay?"

"I will be. I just need to lie low for a bit. Like nine months, apparently."

Bryce swiveled in his chair and laid a gentle hand on his wife's shoulder. "I'm taking you to the doctor."

"I'll be okay. Really."

"I'm sure you will. But you're going to the doctor anyway. We aren't taking risks we don't have to take."

"You're right. We'll go today." Sylvie placed her hand over Bryce's.

Witnessing the couple's connection, Diana couldn't help but smile. She was so glad Sylvie had Bryce. The two of them were so perfect for each other, so focused on love and family. Watching the way they looked at each other, the tender way they touched, made Diana want to believe that maybe such happiness was possible. At least with the right man.

Sylvie focused on Diana. "Let me know about him. Good or bad."

Diana nodded. She'd wanted Sylvie as far away from this case as she could get, but the thought of Sylvie having medical problems with the pregnancy sent a fresh shudder of fear along her nerves. "I'll tell you every detail. And Sylvie?"

"Yes?"

"You and the baby will be okay. Right?"

Sylvie nodded. "I'm sure we will."

Diana nodded, too, but looking at her sister's complexion, she was far from certain.

As soon as Reed stepped out of his car at the construction site where Cord Turner was washing windows, he knew bringing Diana along was a mistake. Just the thought of her being anywhere near a man who might be the Copycat Killer made him want to encase her in bubble wrap and plant her in a jail cell, where he could be sure of her safety.

Maybe Perreth was right. Maybe having Diana around did compromise his thinking. Of course, as he, Diana and Nikki climbed from his car, he realized mistake or not, there wasn't much he could do about it now.

He shook his head and studied the three-story brick mansion jutting up from the shore of Lake Kegonsa. After putting the county sheriff's department on standby, he was confident that if Turner resisted them for whatever reason, they could handle him. And he and Nikki would be able to keep Diana safe. But despite the facts, the situation troubled him far more than he wanted to admit.

Diana and Nikki climbed out of the car, slamming their doors behind them. Stepping over the newly poured curb and gutter, they trudged across construction rubble and over plywood bridging the mud puddles dotting what would eventually be the front yard. An engine roared to life from a dump truck parked at the street. At the side of the house, a bulldozer kicked dust in the air despite the recent rain.

Diana planed her hand over her eyes, blocking the sun. "How do you know he's here?"

"He told Nikki this morning."

She dropped her hand and glanced at Nikki. "You talked to him?"

"I called about getting an estimate. Seems my apartment's windows are in need of a good cleaning." She gave a big proud grin.

Reed almost shook his head. Nikki was just the type who would get a kick out of working undercover some day. He supposed she would, after she got bored with being a detective. If ever there was a woman who had ambitions to experience everything law enforcement had to offer, it was Nikki Valducci.

"So that's all there was to it?" asked Diana.

"You just called and made an appointment and he told you where he was working?"

"Not quite. He said he could stop by after he finished a job for a builder—a house scheduled to close tomorrow. A few calls to title companies, and I now know all the new construction changing hands tomorrow. This was the only builder who admitted to hiring a professional window cleaner. Wa-la, the miracle of police work."

Diana smiled. "I'm impressed."

Reed turned away from Diana and Nikki and devoted his attention to giving the house a once-over. The place looked as if it had a long way to go before anyone could even think about moving in. Of course, once the day of closing approached, he imagined things got done more quickly. Stepping onto the mud-encrusted concrete stoop, Reed froze and knelt down. A wavy-soled footprint was pressed into the dried mud.

"What is it?" Diana leaned over his shoulder.

"Nikki?" He pointed out the footprint. "Take a photo of this, will you?"

Diana knelt down, her hair cascading over one shoulder. The midday sun glinted on her hair, turning it to gold. "It's the same as the tread in the lobby of my building."

Reed's gut hitched. Diana hadn't shared how she felt about having a brother, but he knew. Even if she suspected he could be the Copycat Killer, she wouldn't want to believe it. She would be pulling for him to be innocent with all her heart. Only solid evidence would convince her otherwise, and while a footprint wasn't anywhere near conclusive, it was still evidence. Evidence he wished he didn't have to point out. "It's also similar to the footprint I found in the hotel room last night."

Diana turned to him with horrified eyes. "You think that tread is from the copycat's shoes? How do you know?"

"I don't. It might not mean anything at all. That's the way it is with evidence. Sometimes you don't know what is important until you find something important." He ran a hand through his hair. "That doesn't make any sense, does it?"

"Yes, it does."

"You'll have to explain it to me sometime, then." He glanced from Diana to Nikki and back again. "You two had better wait in the car. This might not mean anything, but I don't want to take a chance. I'll get Turner and bring him out."

Nikki looked up from her camera. "You can't go in there without backup."

"And Diana can't stay alone in the car."

Diana thrust herself to her feet. "Yes, I can. I'll be fine."

He shook his head. This was a mistake. This

whole trip was a mistake. He should have left Diana at the task-force offices. At least there, he knew she'd be safe. "We'll take you back to Madison."

Diana held up a hand. "That's ridiculous. A waste of time. There are construction workers all over the place here. I'll be plenty safe in the car. I'll lock myself in."

He scanned the area. She had a point. Trucks and vans lined the street. Just across the street from the car, three workers ate an early lunch clustered around a van with carpet rolls sticking out the back. Add them to the dump-truck driver, the bulldozer operator, and another silhouette sitting in a van just down the street, and Diana should be safe. With that many people around, someone would have to be crazy to pull anything.

He massaged his aching neck, trying to make himself feel better about the situation. "Lean on the horn if you notice anything out of the ordinary. And I mean *anything*."

She nodded.

"And take these." He reached into his pocket and pulled out the keys. He put them into her hand. "Don't be afraid to just drive away."

"I'll be out of here like a shot." She gave him a teasing smile.

His gut hitched one more time. But this time, fear wasn't the only cause. It had been a long time since she had teased him. A long time since he'd seen that smile that sparkled in her eyes and crinkled her nose. "I mean it, Diana. Be careful."

She nodded. Reversing, she hiked back over the plywood-and-dirt path. He waited until she'd climbed into the car, locked the doors and gave a wave before he turned back to the house.

Having documented the footprint, Nikki followed him through the scarred steel door. A new ornate door of wood and leaded glass leaned against the brick, waiting to be set.

Workers clamored inside, their air hammers popping over the blaring radio. Reed and Nikki stepped gingerly over the paper runner in the foyer that provided a protective pathway over the dusty-gray marble floor. Weaving their way up the partially carpeted staircase, they ventured into three different bedrooms before they finally located Turner working on a giant bay window overlooking the lake.

Turner was built like many ex-cons Reed had known and wished he hadn't. Of average height, like his father, Turner had obviously spent more hours in the prison weight room than Dryden Kane. Tattooed arms like steel pipes stretched the short sleeves of his blue polo shirt. Hard muscle defined his back, tapering to a tool belt hugging a trim waist.

Reed looked down to the ex-con's feet. Work boots. Not a match with the footprints they'd found. Of course, the footprint on the front step was dried. It might not have been made today.

"Cordell Turner?"

The brute tensed and spun around. Light from the window struck the hard planes of his face and glinted off the sharp edge of a razor scraper he held in one fist. He narrowed his eyes on Reed and Nikki. "Who are you? Cops?"

"You expecting police?"

"I'm never expecting police. But with the way you look, you're either a cop or a high-school principal. And I have no idea what a principal would be doing here."

Reed didn't return his smile. "Detective Reed McCaskey and Detective Nikki Valducci of the Madison PD. We need a word with you."

He gestured to the window with the razor. "I'm in a hurry. Got to finish this today. Closing tomorrow."

"It can't wait."

Turner flipped the guard closed on his razor scraper and shoved it into the pouch on his belt. Grabbing a striped towel from a back pocket, he dried his hands. "What about?"

"I need to ask you some questions about your father."

Ice-blue eyes—identical to Kane's—squinted at the reference. "You have the wrong man."

Before they'd left the task-force offices, Reed had looked up Turner's mug shot. He'd been young when it had been taken, and as thin as a rail. But the face was unmistakable—particularly those eyes. "You're the man."

"I don't have a father." He gave a half frown, as if realizing how inane the comment sounded. "I've never met him. My mother never even told me his name."

"Well, I've met him. And I have some questions. So if you'll cooperate, we can make this quick, and you can get back to work."

"And if I don't?"

"I believe cooperating with police is part of the terms of your parole. It would be a shame to go back into the system after only being out two years."

"You think you know all about me, huh?"

"I want to know more."

Turner's jaw hardened. He stared at Reed the way he'd probably stared down fellow convicts.

Reed didn't flinch. Turner might have twenty pounds of muscle on Reed but, in this situation, Reed and Nikki were the ones with the power. If Turner was smart, he'd recognize that.

Finally, Turner let out a long breath. "What do you want to know?"

"Maybe we should step outside." Reed gestured to the men in the master bath, finishing trim. "Unless you want everyone to know your business."

"Fine." He walked to the door.

Reed fell into step behind him and Nikki brought up the rear. So far, so good. But as easy as this encounter had gone, he wasn't about to trust the ex-con.

Not for a second.

They threaded through carpenters, crossed the foyer and filed out the front door. Reed spotted Diana through the passenger window of his car. Letting out a relieved breath, he gave her a nod.

Turner spun to face him, a scowl on his face. "What is she? Some kind of witness? You trying to pin something on me?"

"She's not a witness."

"What is she then?"

Reed hesitated. He didn't want to tell this brute who Diana was. He wanted to slap the cuffs on him and throw him back in the slam where he belonged. Of course if he wasn't the copycat, he shouldn't pose any danger to Diana. And if he was, he already knew about her. "She's your sister."

"Sister?" He clawed a hand through his hair. "I don't have a sister."

"No, you have two."

Turner glanced from Reed to Nikki and back, his eyes as wary as a trapped animal. "What the hell are you talking about? What is going on here?"

Diana approached them. She searched Turner's face. Glancing to Reed, she shook her head.

Reed let out a heavy breath. She didn't remember seeing him. He should have known this wouldn't be that easy. Nothing on this case was easy. "Where were you last night?"

"Why? What the hell do you think I did?"

"I'm asking the questions, Turner."

"Should I be calling a lawyer?"

The last thing Reed wanted Turner to do was lawyer up. After a lawyer entered the fray, it was doubtful Reed could convince the ex-con to admit his name. Of course, he didn't want Turner to know the suggestion bothered him. "You have a lawyer handy?"

"I had a lawyer."

"Ten years ago?" Reed threw his hands out to the side as if Turner was making a stupid mistake. "You can track down your lawyer, waste the rest of the day and a lot of goddamn money, or you can answer a few simple questions and say hello to your sister. Your choice."

Turner narrowed his eyes to icy slits. "Give me your questions, and I'll decide if I want to answer them."

"I gave you the first already. Where were you last night?"

He looked out at the lake beyond the house without really seeming to see it. "I was home."

"Is there anyone who can verify that?"

"I live alone."

"Did you go out at all? Talk to anyone on the phone?"

"No. I ate a frozen pizza and fooled around on eBay."

eBay. He might be able to work with that. "Did you bid on anything?"

"No."

Standing next to him, Nikki scribbled in her notebook.

Reed stroked his chin. "Not much of an alibi."

"I didn't know I would need one. You still haven't told me what the hell this is about."

And he wasn't planning to. Not yet. "How about Saturday night?"

He shook his head. "I don't know. Nothing. Watched TV."

So Turner had no alibi for either the night Nadine Washburn had been abducted nor for the night her body had been displayed in Diana's hotel room. As soon as the autopsy was completed, and they had a time of death, Reed could nail down Turner's story for the time of her murder. So far,

Cordell Turner wasn't off to a good start. "You said you don't know who your father is."

"That's right."

"Have you ever visited the Banesbridge Correctional Facility?"

"No."

"Have you ever visited the Wisconsin Secure Detention Facility or the Grantsville Correctional Facility?"

"No. You know I can't associate with cons. The parole?"

"How about before you were in prison?"

"When I was a kid?"

"Yes."

"What are you saying? My father is in prison?" He glanced at Diana for the first time, as if looking to her for help.

"Answer my question."

"No. I don't remember ever setting foot in a prison. Not until the day I was sentenced."

"Tell me about that."

"Nothing to tell."

"You were convicted for manslaughter."

"I got in a fight. I killed a man." He shrugged a shoulder, as if it weren't a big deal. Maybe to him, killing wasn't. "I served my time."

"And that happened in Milwaukee?"

"Was that a question? You know it did."

"What brought you to the Madison area?"

"There's nothing in my parole that says I can't live in Madison. I informed the court of my move. I dotted the i's and crossed the t's."

"But you grew up in Milwaukee. Everyone you knew was in Milwaukee. Why the move?"

"I wanted to branch out, find some new friends."

Reed stared the con down. He needed his smart-ass sarcasm like he needed a hole in the head. "You're not doing yourself any favors with that attitude."

Turner expelled a breath. "What does my move from Milwaukee have to do with anything?"

"Do you expect me to believe you moved to Madison for no reason whatsoever?"

"No. I had a good reason for moving here. But it didn't have anything to do with some father I don't even know, if that's what you're getting at." He tossed Diana a glare. "Or any sisters."

"So what does it have to do with?"

He balled his hands into fists, as if preparing to slug his way out. "I've cooperated enough. Now it's time for *you* to give *me* some answers. Who the hell do you think is my father?"

Reed focused on the hard lines of Turner's face. He might as well tell him, watch for his reaction. "Dryden Kane."

His eyes flared wide. Red crept up his neck. "You're full of it."

"It's true." Diana's voice rang steady, despite the tangle of emotion playing across her face. "Dryden Kane is our biological father. He was involved with your mother when they were both teenagers back in a little town up north called Oshishobee. Before he married my mother."

Turner swung to face her. "Bull."

"I didn't want to believe it either. Neither did Sylvie, my twin. But we're his daughters. And you...you look just like him. You look so much like him."

"Eff you. All of you." He spun around and strode for the house.

Nikki stepped after him. "We're not finished."

"I'm finished," he shouted over his shoulder. "You want to talk? You can talk to my lawyer. She's in the book. Meredith Unger."

Reed's heart jolted against his ribs. Here he was looking for a connection to Kane, and Turner had just served it up burning from the grill. Nodding to Nikki, he glanced over his shoulder, meeting Diana's wide eyes. "Get back in the car and lock the doors."

Diana answered with an urgent nod.

"If anything happens, promise me you'll get the hell out of here."

She paused.

"Promise me."

"I promise."

"Go."

She trotted in the direction of the car.

Pushing away the hitch in his gut, Reed tore his gaze from her and made for the house. "We're not finished, Turner."

The ex-con didn't slow. He bounded past the dump truck, up the shallow steps and pushed open the front door, disappearing inside.

Reed broke into a jog. Nikki fell in beside him. Turner had something to hide, all right. And if the brute didn't come clean, Reed would haul him downtown. It shouldn't be too hard to find something to get him on. One dirty look and Reed could bust his ass for parole violation.

He pushed aside the image of Diana. He knew she'd wanted to believe her brother was clean. He could tell just by the way she'd leaned toward him when trying to explain their family history, as if she were willing him to come around, to recognize the family bond. Reed hated to be the one to point out the futility of her hopes. But he'd dealt with ex-cons far more than she had. He knew them. And once dirty, these guys never really cleaned up their acts.

He and Nikki squeezed past the truck and reached the stairs. The dump truck roared in his ears. As he climbed the steps, he glanced back for Diana.

Half the distance to the car, she picked her

way across the plywood. A few more feet and she'd be safe.

He turned back to the house. Nikki pulled in front of him. She reached the door. He took the steps two at a time to catch up. Behind him the dump truck roared. Louder. Closer. As if it was bearing down.

He spun around.

The truck's massive grill rushed toward him. Tires churning over boards, it surged through mud and up the steps.

It was trying to run them down.

Reed plunged forward. He threw out his hands, shoving Nikki in the back, pushing her through the door.

Wood splintered behind them. Metal crumpled. Brick crashed and debris spewed. He hurtled forward, vaulting over Nikki, trying to break his fall with his outstretched hands.

His skull smacked against gray marble and the world went dark.

Chapter Thirteen

A crash shook the air.

Diana's breath caught in her throat. She whirled around in time to see the dump truck lodge itself in the front door, brick crumbling around it. "Reed!"

She raced for the house, her feet stumbling over rocks and dirt before she'd even made the decision to move. The last she'd seen him, he'd been climbing the steps—steps now under the truck's wide tires. She didn't know what she'd do, but she had to do something. She had to stop the truck. She had to find Reed. She had to make sure he was okay.

Please, let him be okay.

She pushed her legs to move. She had to run faster. She had to reach Reed before it was too late.

Ahead, the truck's wheels quit spinning. The driver's door opened and a man dressed in a navy mechanic's jumpsuit leaped out. A ski mask covered his head, leaving only small openings for his eyes and mouth.

Urgency pounded through Diana's chest, as hot as flame. She couldn't let him reach the door. Reed could be hurt. Defenseless. She couldn't let this man hurt him further.

The man in the ski mask circled the truck. Reaching the back bed, he brandished a knife.

And headed straight for her.

REED'S HEAD CLANGED, the sensation more a feeling than a sound. Confusion clouded his brain. Pain sat heavy on the back of his neck. He struggled to clear his mind. He had to pull himself together. He had to think.

How long had he been lying here?

He lifted his head, then let it fall throbbing back to the floor. He recognized the house. The construction around him. The marble floor cool and gritty under his cheek. He remembered talking to Turner. He remembered the ex-con's comment about his attorney. Meredith Unger. And then... the truck.

He jolted upright. His head spun with the sudden movement. His stomach lurched. Dust hung in the air, making it hard to see. He couldn't have been out long. The dust would have cleared. Help would have come.

"What the hell happened?" As if summoned from his thoughts, the voice echoed from above. Footsteps clattered down stairs. "Are you okay?"

A groan stirred from somewhere near his knees. Nikki.

"I need some help here." He clawed through debris. His hand touched her tangled hair. "Nikki?"

"What?"

Three construction workers thundered down the stairs, gaping at the truck's nose protruding through the crumbling doorway.

Nikki pulled herself up into a sitting position with little help, eyes barely open.

Thank God. "You all right?"

"Peachy." Eyes closed, she swiped at her face, trying to clear away Sheetrock dust and rubble. "I can't see a damn thing. Did you get him?"

Him. The truck driver.

Reed forced himself to his feet. His legs and neck ached to high heaven. He shook his head, only increasing the pounding in his brain. He had to make his mind work. He had to clear the confusion from his brain. The truck driver was still out there.

And so was Diana.

Red-hot fear flushed through him. He staggered, almost losing his balance. He grabbed the banister, willing himself to stay upright.

A worker reached out a steadying hand. "You'd better sit down."

He shrugged the guy off. He didn't have time to sit down. He didn't have time to think. He had to get out of the damn house. He had to find Diana.

The truck's grill lodged in the open door, the structure around the portal broken and crumbling. He'd get around it or find another way out. He couldn't leave Diana to face the driver of the truck alone. The driver he knew in his gut was the Copycat Killer.

He spun away from the front door. Several hallways branched off the left side of the foyer, the dining room, the kitchen, and who knew what else. Somewhere in there was the path to the garage exit. But judging from the size of the house, he might have to negotiate a maze to get there.

He didn't have time.

He raced for the front of the house. Shoes crunching on bits of drywall and glass, he skidded over the marble floor and slammed through French doors and into the dining room.

Three double-hung windows peered out on the front yard, their panes so caked with construction dust, he couldn't see a thing through them. He chose the closest. Turning the brass lock, he grasped the bottom sash, pushed it up and tore it from the frame. Next he pulled the storm free, letting it fall to the floor, glass shattering. Bracing himself on the window frame, he thrust his foot through the screen, kicking out the nylon mesh and climbing through the opening. His feet hit dirt. He scrambled upright. Pulling his Glock from his shoulder holster, he raced around the dump truck.

His car sat by the curb where he'd left it, but Diana wasn't there.

His mind stuttered. Alarm knifed through him. She had to be here. She had to.

A shout echoed from down the street.

He ran in the direction of the sound. Clearing the row of vans and trucks lining the street, he spotted a cluster of workers. In the middle of the men, a flash of blond hair caught the sunlight.

His heart pounded high in his chest. He ducked back behind the trucks and ran parallel to the street. Drawing closer, he caught a better view. A man stood behind her, face covered with a ski mask. One of his gloved hands clutched Diana's hair. The other held a knife to her throat.

"Hold on here. You don't want to hurt her." One of the construction workers held up his hands, as if trying to calm the masked man.

Crouching low behind the vehicles, Reed ran as fast as he could. He had to get behind the masked man without giving himself away. If he could take him by surprise, he could keep Diana from getting hurt.

"Why don't you just let her go?" the construction worker continued. "Take my van and get out of here? It's right there. The keys are in the switch."

Reed willed him to keep talking, keep offering alternatives. Anything to keep the masked man busy until Reed could get into position. He slipped between the bumpers of a panel van and a pickup, leading with his pistol.

He could see Diana's face from here. Chalk-white, she looked remarkably calm and determined. Jaw set. Eyes on fire.

The guy in the ski mask inched closer to the offered van. Hand still tangled in Diana's hair, he dragged her with him.

Reed wasn't going to let the bastard get her inside. He wasn't going to let him take her. He raised the gun, pointing the barrel at the man's head.

It was a tricky shot. Too much could go wrong. A few inches to one side or the other, a sudden movement, and he'd miss. He hesitated.

The masked man grasped the handle of the driver's door and opened it. To get Diana into the van, the guy would have to lower the knife. He'd have to use both hands to heft her inside. And when he did, Reed would be ready. He would have the shot he wanted.

"Let her go. Just take the van." The construction

worker stepped toward Diana and the masked man. One more step and he'd be directly between Reed and the man.

He took another step, obscuring Reed's view.

Damn, damn, damn.

Suddenly the self-declared hero sprang at the masked man.

No. Reed lunged between the cars. "Police! Drop your weapon!"

He couldn't shoot. Not without hitting the construction worker. Not without hitting Diana.

The masked man thrust his knife at the construction worker.

The man grunted and doubled over. He staggered toward the vehicle.

The masked man leaped into the van, dragging Diana with him. She struggled, twisting, clawing at his arms and face.

"Police! Put down your weapon! Now! Now! Now!" The bastard wasn't going to get away. He wasn't going to take Diana. Swinging his aim to one of the van's tires, Reed pulled the trigger.

Pop.

Air hissed from the tire. Pop. He took out another tire. He lunged toward the van, dodging around the wounded worker.

The masked man released Diana's hair. He gave her a shove.

Reed lunged for her, falling to his knees, helping break her fall.

The van roared down the street, bucking on two flat tires.

DIANA FOLLOWED A NURSE between the white curtains dividing a cluster of the emergency room's examination cubicles. Her scalp throbbed, the bruises on her knees from her fall hurt with each step, and she doubted she would ever stop shaking. All the same, she had no doubts that she was the luckiest woman on earth.

Thanks to Reed and a construction worker she'd never met.

The nurse paused at the last cubicle and pulled the curtain aside. "You got a visitor. Doctor should be back soon."

Reed smiled at Diana from the hospital bed. Sitting up, he swung his legs over the edge. "Hi."

Diana couldn't hide her relief at seeing him. After the man in the ski mask had shoved her into his arms and sped down the street, she'd held Reed so tightly, she didn't think she'd ever be able to let go. Even now, the urge to sink onto the bed beside him and cuddle into his arms throbbed inside her like a hunger.

She let out a long breath and offered a shaky smile. "Hi."

"You lie down until the doctor gets here. Or she's likely to check you into a room," the nurse admonished. Without enforcing the order, she turned around and bustled back down the hall.

"Check me into a room?" Reed muttered. "Not if she can't catch me."

"You'd better do what she says." Diana stepped closer to the bed. She'd been so scared. Even after all she'd been through in the cabin last fall, she'd never been as panicked as when she'd seen that truck smash into the house in the precise spot where Reed had been just moments before. Even when the masked driver had pressed that knife to her throat, she hadn't been as frightened. "How are you feeling?"

He held up a hand and gingerly touched the bandage. Red and purple bruising eked out around the bandage's edge. "Like I've been hit by a truck."

"I guess you were." She fought the urge to reach out and touch him, too, to make sure he really was all right. She hated how pale he looked. How weak. She couldn't stand the idea of him being injured.

Of course, he could be dead.

The thought lodged in her chest. From the time she was eighteen, Reed had always been there. Shielding her from her father, encouraging her to move out, go to college. And as adamant as she was about taking care of herself, living her own life, the thought of him not in the world, somewhere, was worse than dying herself.

"Have you seen Nikki?"

Diana managed to nod. "She was released a little more than an hour ago."

"Then why the hell am I still here?" He made a forward motion, as if about to get up and walk out.

Diana pressed her palm against his chest, pushing him back to the bed. "You have a concussion. That's why."

"I'll survive. It isn't like I've never had a concussion before."

"Exactly. That's why they aren't going to let you out of here until they know you're okay."

"How about the construction worker?"

"The nurse wouldn't tell me the details, but she did say he's out of surgery and doing well." She'd already arranged to send him flowers, and as soon as the hospital would let her, she'd visit him. She owed her life to that man. He was a true hero.

Reed looked at his watch. "At this rate, *he's* going to be out of here before they release me."

"Patience."

"I know. It's never been my strong suit." He shrugged, as if tossing off his frustration. Meeting her eyes, he touched the back of her hand. "I can't tell you how glad I am that worker was there. That you're okay."

Shivers traveled up her arm. She knew she should pull her arm away, step away from the bed. But God help her, she didn't want to.

"I'm so sorry, Diana. I never should have left you. I should have—"

"Stop it." She couldn't stand to hear one more word. "It was my idea to stay in the car. *My idea*."

"I shouldn't have let you."

"You couldn't have stopped me."

He ran a hand over his face. "My God, listen to us. After all this, we're still arguing about the same thing." He glanced at the bed beside him, an invitation to sit down.

She lowered herself to the mattress. He was so close, she could feel the heat of him. If she leaned just a few inches to the side, she would be in his arms. The tremor that had shaken her legs and stomach since this whole thing had started moved upward, lodging under her ribs.

He met her eyes, his gaze dark and intense. "When I realized you were out there, with that maniac…" His voice grew gruff and trailed off.

"Don't." She knew what he was about to say, but she didn't want him to continue. She didn't want him to say another word. It took too much effort to fight her emotions. Too much strength to keep the image of that truck bearing down on him from her mind. If he voiced his feelings, she knew she wouldn't be able to keep the wall between them in place, the skin that separated her from him.

He shook his head. "I don't know what I would have done."

She turned to him, covering his lips with her hand, stemming the flow of words. "Please, don't."

He clasped her hand in his. Holding it in front of him, he pressed his lips to her palm.

Shivers shimmered up her arm and through her body. She opened her mouth to tell him to stop, but no sound came.

He kissed her again, his lips caressing the inside of her wrist. Then the inside of her forearm.

She couldn't speak, couldn't move. All she could do was stare into his dark eyes as his kisses flayed open her heart.

"I convinced them to let you out of here." Nikki's voice cut the quiet. She threw the curtain back.

Diana pulled her arm from Reed's grasp.

"Oh, sorry. I'll come back later."

The heat of blood rushed into Diana's cheeks. She didn't care what Nikki had seen. Simple embarrassment, she could live with. But the knowledge that one look from Reed, one touch, one kiss, and she was willing to give up everything she'd worked so hard for shook her to her toes.

She jolted up from the bed. "No need. Did you say the doctor is releasing Reed?"

Nikki gave them both a wary look. "She should be in any second to do just that. I convinced her that you have a hard head."

Reed nodded. "True enough." He leaned down to grab his shoes, gripping the bed for balance.

Diana reached out to steady him, trying to brace herself against the feel of his solid arm under her hand.

Nikki's expression turned to worry. "I hope springing you isn't premature. You look a little dizzy."

Reed straightened, holding the shoes. "I'm fine."

"You'd better be. You're going to need all the strength you can get. The lieutenant wants to see you downtown at the district office. The place is flooded with FBI in addition to our own and the county sheriff's department, and we're getting headlines on all the cable news networks. In other words, all hell has broken loose."

"Funny. I thought it already had." Reed slipped one shoe on. "So what's the cause of the new wave?"

Alarm buzzed through Diana's blood. Nikki and Reed might be able to throw humor into the mix— they might even need to, since they dealt with life and death as part of their jobs daily—but Diana wasn't so calm and collected.

Nikki paused. There was no humor in her dark eyes now. "The Copycat has another victim."

Another victim.

Images of Nadine Washburn's body flashed through Diana's mind. She felt helpless. Sick.

Reed leveled a serious look on Nikki. "When?"

"We think sometime last night. Obviously after he dumped Nadine Washburn's body. Her husband was out of town. When he returned this afternoon, he found their two-month-old baby in the house alone."

"The baby?" A baby without a mother. A baby lying alone in her crib for hours. Diana couldn't breathe.

"Yeah, but that's not the kicker."

There was more? Her legs felt weak. She leaned against the wall.

Reed pulled on his second shoe. "What else?"

"The husband. He's the governor's son. The brass, the press, the whole damn world is going crazy."

Diana understood Nikki's concern. That much media coverage and pressure would doubtlessly affect her and Reed's investigation. But that wasn't the important thing to Diana. She didn't care who the husband was or what kind of influence his father wielded. The baby was the important thing.

The baby was the only thing that mattered.

Chapter Fourteen

Reed watched Diana through the office-door window as he waited for the lieutenant to finish his phone call. She sat very still in the corner, watching the flurry around her. The district office was three times as busy as usual. Even with many of the officers already moved to new task-force offices and more out working the streets, the infusion of brass, politicos and FBI nearly overran the building and spilled onto the sidewalk.

Of course, he doubted they would fit on the sidewalks with the throng of media hovering outside.

The lieutenant slammed down his ancient corded phone and peered at Reed through frameless glasses. He'd always looked tired, even on a good day. But today he looked more exhausted than usual. And although he was already nearly bald, Reed could swear he lost more hair with each day the copycat case went unsolved.

Reed had known as soon as he'd walked into the district office that this was no ordinary meeting. Not that a meeting would ever be ordinary with a serial killer on the loose. But judging from the hushed and fervent looks he'd received from people who would be in the know, he sensed this meeting was about him. And that he wasn't going to like it. "What did you want to talk to me about?"

"We have some problems with this investigation. Problems I need to address."

"What kind of problems?"

"Lack-of-result problems."

Reed tried his best not to roll his eyes. He wished the lieutenant would have the balls to come out and say what he meant. "What exactly do you mean, lack-of-result problems?"

"We need an arrest."

"Don't you think I would arrest the son of a bitch if we had any idea who he is?"

"You've been working this case too long not to know who he is."

Reed almost did a double take on that one. The lieutenant knew what kind of evidence they'd found; he knew the current facts of the case; he knew Reed would give anything to nail the copycat. "I can't pull evidence out of my ass."

He knew he shouldn't be talking that way to the lieutenant of detectives, but the inference that

Reed had been wasting time all these months chapped him so badly he wouldn't be able to sit for a week.

"I expect results. The captain expects results. The chief expects results. The goddamn mayor expects results. And I can promise you the governor expects results."

He forgot the voters. Politicians always did. And even though the lieutenant wasn't voted into office, he had always had a bit of the politician about him.

Reed drew a deep breath and let the air between them cool. Getting hotheaded wouldn't help anyone. And provoking his boss would do even less good. "So what are you saying?"

The lieutenant adjusted his glasses and narrowed his eyes on Reed. "You know how it works. Someone has to take responsibility for the lack of results."

"And you want it to be me?"

He turned and paced across the tiny office. "You've been spending an inordinate amount of time investigating Dryden Kane's involvement in this, and you don't have any leads to show for it."

A cramp seized the back of Reed's neck. Something stank, and it wasn't just sewage seeping into ceiling tiles. "You've been talking to Perreth."

The lieutenant shook his head. "I know he's not

an objective source. I know there's bad blood between you. This isn't about anything Perreth said."

"Maybe not. But I'm willing to bet Perreth's sabotage is a contributing factor. Hell, maybe that's why you insisted Perreth be part of the task force in the first place."

"I'm not your enemy, McCaskey."

"No? It sure looks like it from here."

He splayed his hands out in front of him, as if beseeching Reed to understand. "This is the governor's daughter-in-law we're talking about. *Governor Copeland's daughter-in-law.*"

"I've heard." Reed felt horrible for Cerise Copeland, her husband and her baby. Hell, he even felt bad for the governor. But it wasn't as if the family she'd married into made her more important than Nadine Washburn or the three women killed last autumn.

Of course in the real world of politics and media hype, it did. The other four women had been lucky they were blond-haired and blue-eyed. If they'd been minorities, they would have been truly invisible to the political and media powers that be.

"You know how much sensationalism goes with a serial-killer case. When you throw in the governor's daughter-in-law and some unproven connection to Dryden Kane…" The lieutenant threw his hands in the air.

Reed leveled him with a dispassionate stare. He didn't have time to worry about the political end of this mess. He'd leave those ambitions to Nikki, Perreth and the lieutenant himself. He just wanted to find a killer. "I know more about this case than anyone. I have my finger on what every member of the task force is working on. I can talk to the feds, the guys from the sheriff's department. I make the whole thing work. If you want, take over the media part of this. Or give it to Perreth. I don't care. Just let me handle the investigative end."

The lieutenant blew out a long breath. Slipping his glasses off his nose, he swiped at one of the lenses with his tie before putting them back on. "I'm sorry, Reed."

Reed shut his eyes. "You can't do this."

"Go home. Get some rest. I'm sure you haven't slept in days."

He opened his eyes and peered through the window, focusing on Diana. The lieu might be able to pull the investigation out from under him and hand it to someone else, but Reed wasn't about to trust Diana's protection to whatever officer his boss drew out of a hat. "What if I reassign myself to a different role?"

The lieutenant arched his thin brows. "What role?"

"Bodyguard."

DIANA SAT ON THE OTTOMAN she'd slid beside Reed's living-room couch. It had taken ten minutes to convince him to lie back on the pillows she'd mounded beneath his back and head, and ten more to convince him to let her check him out. If he insisted on being any more difficult, she was going to bop him one. "Look straight ahead."

"Yes, Doctor."

Turning on the flashlight, she aimed the beam just past his left ear.

His pupil scoped to a small dot amid the rich brown iris.

"How am I doing?" He squinted against the light.

"I have to check the other eye." She pointed the flashlight away from his face.

"I'm fine, Diana."

"I'll let you know if you're fine or not. Now let me see your right eye." She went through the same routine with the light on the right side.

"I told you."

"Do you still have the headache?"

"The doctor said that might take a while to go away."

"I'll take that as a yes."

He groaned.

"Watch it. Irritability is also a symptom of concussion."

"Only if it's something new."

She couldn't help but smile.

"You don't have to hover over me, you know. I really am okay."

She knew he was physically okay, except for the bruises and headache. But emotionally okay? That was another question. "I can't believe your lieutenant is making you the fall guy."

He shrugged one shoulder, as if it wasn't a big deal.

The gesture didn't fool Diana. Not for a second. Reed would probably choose a headache and ringing in the ears over being taken off the case. As for her, the worry over Reed's career and the fate of the case was tempered only by her relief that he would finally be able to get some rest. "How does your head feel? Do you need more Tylenol?"

He reached up, capturing her hand. "I mean it, Diana. I brought you here because I don't trust Perreth to find someone competent to protect you. You don't have to take care of me."

"So you're allowed to take care of me, but not the other way around?"

A sheepish grin spread over his face, but he didn't let go of her hand. "All right. Point taken. I would love more pain pills."

She extricated her hand from his. Tingles stole up her arm and turned to warm flutters in her chest as she walked into Reed's immaculate and hardly used kitchen. She grabbed the bottle of Tylenol and ran a glass of water from the tap, trying her best not to remember the last time she'd been in Reed's apartment. The day before their wedding—a wedding that had never taken place.

She'd come so far since that time. She hoped she'd put those kinds of doubts and fears behind her for good. The memory of how afraid she'd been that Reed would find out who her father was, that it would change the way he felt about her, made her cringe inside.

She stepped into the doorway to the living room. Pausing, she let her gaze fall on Reed. Her heartbeat quickened, the pounding irregular and jumbled in her chest. Seeing him had always done that to her, made her feel weak, needy.

Leaning against the pillows, he stared out the picture window, the streetlights' glow falling on his face.

She carried the water and tablets to the couch. Handing them to him, she stood back and watched him pop them into his mouth and drink down the water. "Now was that so hard?" She reached out for the glass.

Instead of handing it to her, Reed trapped her hand in his. "Sit down."

She hesitated. She must have been crazy agreeing to stay at his apartment. Sure, his building was security locked. Sure, she could watch him, make sure he was recovering properly from his blow to the head. But she didn't have to think back to his kisses in the hospital to know it was a bad idea. She only had to look at him from across the room to experience the confusion he created in her.

"Haven't you ever heard of bedside manner? Yours needs some work."

She shook her head. God knew with his fingers wrapped around hers, her knees felt too weak to stand much longer anyway. She lowered herself to the ottoman.

"Don't tell me. When you were growing up, you always wanted to be a doctor."

She forced out the breath she didn't know she was holding. She had to admit that being safe in his apartment, talking about silly things felt good. Normal. Something she hadn't had a taste of in what seemed like a very long while. "Nope. Never wanted to be a doctor."

"A nurse?"

"No."

"What then?"

She allowed a smile to lift the corners of her lips. "A superhero."

"Really? That's the reason for your office decor?"

She nodded. She'd decorated her home office

with female action figures and posters. She'd never realized she'd never told Reed why.

"So who did you want to be?"

"Wonder Woman. Her name is Diana, you know."

"I guess I should have figured that one out."

"She's strong. She can fly. No one messes with her."

"Or if they do, they're toast." He gave her a sympathetic smile and she knew he was thinking of Ed Gale.

"Right. It was a nice fantasy, to be that powerful. Who am I kidding? It's still a nice fantasy." No more Dryden Kane. No worries about protecting the people she loved. No more helplessness and fear.

She shook her head. Dwelling on fantasies would get her nowhere. She glanced at Reed. "I suppose you always wanted to be a police officer."

"Not until junior high. Before that I just wanted to be a big brother."

"As in part of the group Big Brothers Big Sisters?"

"No. As in having a lot of younger siblings."

Diana had to raise her brows at that. Reed's parents were both doctors. To this day, they were very involved with Doctors Without Borders, traveling around the world to help people in need. As dedicated as they were to their chosen professions, they'd done well to raise one child, let alone more. "How many is a lot?"

"A dozen or so."

A short laugh escaped her lips. She pressed a hand over her mouth.

"I know. A little unrealistic. But I dream big."

"I always thought being an only child had its perks. I didn't have to share my toys. I got all the attention." Of course, she'd gotten all the bad attention as well as the good, but that was another matter. "Why did you want so many siblings?"

"My parents were always trying to help other people. Through their work. Through charities." He stroked his thumb along her index finger. "I guess I just wanted to be like them. I wanted someone to need me, too."

Her throat pinched, making it hard to swallow.

"As it turned out, I never got those brothers and sisters. I never knew what it was like to be really needed. Not until the job. Not until you."

His words cut into her defenses. Into her self-control. She'd never understood before. Never even considered why he always took care of her. Only that it was a part of him. A part she couldn't change.

She pulled her hand from his grasp and pushed up from the ottoman. Stepping to the window, she stared out into the blackness. "I can't need you that way, Reed. Not anymore."

"I know." The couch rustled. His footsteps padded across the carpet behind her. "I didn't really understand that before. Not until these past few days. Not until I got the chance to see how strong you are."

Chills rose along her arms and over her back. It felt as if she'd waited forever to hear him say those words, even longer to believe them herself. But though she'd always envisioned this moment would make things clear in her mind, she couldn't have been more wrong. Feeling Reed's heat behind her, hearing his voice, aching to be in his arms made her feel weaker than ever. "What does that mean? For us?"

"Is there an us?"

She shook her head. She was so confused. So unsure. She felt as if she were walking the edge of a cliff and one wrong step would send her falling into oblivion. "I don't know."

"I want there to be an us. More than you know." He raised a hand to her face. Touching her chin with a finger, he turned her head toward him.

She turned her whole body to face him, afraid to think, afraid to breathe.

"I've learned a lot in these past few days, Diana. But the most important thing I learned was how badly I need you."

She closed her eyes. His words washed over her. Words she never thought she'd hear. Words that gathered in her chest and filled her with warmth.

Filled her with power.

She took a step. Into his arms. Into his heat.

He brought his lips down on hers. Hungry. Demanding. Showing his need. His kiss at once familiar and totally new.

She pressed her body against the hard length of him. Devoured his kiss as he devoured hers. She'd stepped over the edge and was falling, but she didn't care. She didn't care about anything but the warmth of his body and the taste of his mouth.

He skimmed his hands up her sides, taking her shirt with him. He slipped it over her head, then circled his hands around her back to unhook her bra.

Cool air caressed her breasts and puckered her nipples.

He moved his hands up over her ribs and cupped her in his palms.

Diana arched her back, pushing her breasts into the caress of his hands. She brought her hands to his shirt. Forcing her fingers to work, she slipped his buttons free and spread the fabric away from his chest.

His touch felt so good, so right. So much about the feel of him was the same. Warm. Safe. Yet so much had changed.

So much about her had changed.

She ran her hands under his shirt, soaking in the texture of his skin, the rasp of the hair sprinkled in the center of his chest. She wanted to recapture what they'd had. The passion. The heat. Yet she wanted something different. Something elusive. She could taste it on her tongue.

Heat shimmered in her chest, building and strengthening like kindling fire. She moved down his body, sliding kisses over his chest, his belly, tracing the trail of hair down to where it disappeared into his waistband. She settled on her knees. Raising trembling hands, she unfastened his belt and lowered his fly.

He buried his hands in her hair, his fingers massaging her sore scalp in a gentle caress.

She pulled his slacks down his legs, taking his briefs with them. She'd been so young when they'd met, so young the first time she'd touched him, the first time they'd made love. She'd taken his body for granted. The strength of it, the power of it, the responsiveness to her touch. She didn't take it for granted anymore.

She brushed her fingers up the underside of his shaft, lifting him, bringing him closer to her mouth. She let her breath wash over him.

He pulsed with movement at her touch. A moan rumbled through his chest.

She wanted to spend all night touching him, tasting him, reveling in the way he moved under her caress. She wanted to savor the clear evidence of how much he wanted her. How much he needed her.

Warmth surged through her, pooling between her thighs. She'd never felt so desperate for him, yet so sure of her own strength, her own power. She wanted more. She wanted to show him how she felt. She wanted to see how he felt about her.

Slipping her tongue between her lips, she flicked up the same path her hand had taken. Reaching his tip, she slid her lips over him, taking him fully into her mouth.

He filled her, pressing against her tongue, moving down her throat. She took him as far into her mouth as she could, then slid her lips back to his tip.

A shudder shook his body. He cupped her head in his hands as if he needed to hold on.

She circled his thighs, each with one arm. She could feel his muscles tremble, feel him thrust forward each time she took him into her mouth. She arched her back, thrusting her breasts forward against his thighs. As she sank her lips over him, her nipples rubbed the rough hair on his legs. Tingles spread over her skin in waves.

He gripped her shoulders, as if desperate to hang on, desperate to keep control.

But he wasn't in control.

Heat surged through her. She let him slide from

her lips, cupping him between her breasts, moving against him. The friction of his skin and hair against her nipples made her want to cry out. It made her want more.

"Diana." Reed's voice sounded low, gruff with need. "We need to slow down. I can't take much more."

She smiled, wanting to send him over the edge, wanting to feel him totally lose control. But he was right. Not yet.

She rose from her knees, skimming kisses up his body until she reached his lips.

"Come to bed with me. I want to show you some things, too."

She nodded, not sure if her voice would work, not wanting to talk.

He took her hand. Together they walked into his bedroom. Light streamed in from the living room, shining across the white span of comforter covering the bed.

Reed hesitated in the doorway. He stepped back toward the living room, away from her.

Cool air rushed around her, chilling her skin where his heat used to be. "Where are you going?"

He gestured to the living room. "The light's kind of bright, don't you think?"

She shook her head. She didn't want him to step away from her, even for a second. She didn't want to be in the dark again. "I think it's perfect. I want to see your eyes."

He grinned and swept her back into his arms. Moving his hands down her sides, he quickly removed her jeans. Cupping her buttocks, he lifted her up against him, kissing her long and hard before lowering her to the bed and sitting beside her. "Lie back. Let me show you how *I* feel."

She wanted to let him show her. She wanted to let him have his way, take her places she'd only visited in dreams. But not now. Not yet.

Putting her palm on his chest, she pushed him back onto the mattress. "Later. I'm not finished." She straddled his hips, moving against his hard length before sinking onto him.

He filled her, stretched her so exquisitely she had to catch her breath. Then she started moving, her breasts swaying over him.

He caught her nipples in his mouth, kissing her, suckling her. All the while he watched her, his eyes soaking her in. And as the pressure inside her crested and broke, she felt like the most powerful woman on earth.

Chapter Fifteen

When Diana woke to morning sunlight stretching through the window, the bed next to her was empty. She tossed back the covers and forced her sore muscles to function, crawling from the bed. The fatigue in her legs felt delicious. And the redness coloring her skin from cheeks to inner thighs caused by the stubble on Reed's face made her flush with heat.

She'd never felt so powerful as she had last night. She wanted to hold on to it. She wanted it to never end.

She climbed out of bed, her legs wobbling the first few steps. She knew she should take it slow, that she should find out for certain things had changed before she charged headlong into her feelings for Reed. But the giddiness flowing through her blood like champagne was too delicious not to enjoy. She had believed her relationship with Reed was over. To discover it didn't have to be made her want to sing.

She took a quick hot shower, and pulled a clean pair of jeans and a T-shirt out of her suitcase; but, although she swore she'd packed another pair of underwear, she couldn't find them anywhere. She hoped she hadn't left them in the hotel room.

The hotel room where they'd found Nadine.

Suppressing a shiver, she pushed Nadine from her mind. She needed a rest from death and blood and fear. Even if it was just a day, she yearned to focus on normal things. The elation bubbling in her blood. The satisfied ache between her legs. Reed.

She dressed. Hair hanging wet to her shoulders, she padded out into the living room on bare feet.

Reed sat in the dinette with his back to her. Hunched over with his elbows on the table, he concentrated on a stack of paper in front of him.

She peered over his shoulder, recognizing the missing persons reports she hadn't yet finished going through. The weight of reality settled back into her bones. "I should have known you were working."

He looped an arm around her waist and gathered her into his arms. "You smell so good."

"I took a shower."

"You smelled even better last night."

Pleasure flushed through her. She wished all she had to think about was how good his arms felt around her. She wished all they had to talk about was their desire for each other. But that wasn't the case. It couldn't be. Not with Cerise Copeland in the copycat's clutches. Not with a baby longing for its mother.

And not under the shadow of Dryden Kane.

She looked down at the forms on the table. "Want some help with those?"

"Sure." He handed her a stack of forms.

She slipped into the chair next to Reed's and ran her gaze over the now familiar headings in each box. This woman was from outside Dane County, an area along a lake built up with upscale homes. She'd left the house to meet friends for dinner in Madison before a concert at the Overture Center. She'd never arrived.

Diana glanced at the boxes detailing her clothing. Her sister had reported she'd been dressed for a fancy restaurant. A little black dress. Expensive shoes. And a diamond-and-emerald necklace.

Diana's breath lodged in her throat.

Reed looked up from his stack of reports. "What is it?"

She tried to answer, but her mind was numb. It

couldn't be true. It had to be some kind of mistake. She couldn't be so incredibly blind.

She'd read about it in the research she'd done on serial killers. How they often kept victims' jewelry as souvenirs of their kills. How some monsters gave this jewelry to women in their lives, their wives, daughters, girlfriends. How every time they looked at the jewelry, they could relive the murder, they could assert their dominance over the woman they supposedly loved.

She handed the report to Reed and forced the words from her lips. "Her necklace. Emeralds and diamonds. White gold. It's the one Louis gave me."

"I CAN'T BELIEVE IT. He was always real polite. Quiet like. Never gave me no trouble."

Reed gripped the search warrant in a fist and waited for the manager of Diana's apartment building to flip through his entire collection of keys to find the one that fit Ingersoll's door.

He couldn't believe it either. Couldn't believe he'd been so stupid. Couldn't believe he'd ignored his gut about Diana's neighbor. Here he'd been trying to protect Diana, and he'd missed the small fact that her neighbor was a serial killer.

The paper crumpled in his hand.

He glanced back at the officers around him.

Weapons at the ready, they watched for his lead. They were fairly certain Ingersoll wasn't home. He should be out making deliveries for the food company. But it didn't hurt to be sure.

The lieutenant hadn't wanted Reed to have any part of taking Ingersoll down, but he'd relented enough to give Reed the job of executing the search warrant. At least it was something. Truth be told, he couldn't blame the lieu. With the scent of Diana still swirling in his mind, he'd rather kill Ingersoll than look at him.

The manager slipped another key in the lock. This time the knob turned under his hand. "Here it is."

"Thank you, sir. Now I need you to go back downstairs." Reed nodded to one of the officers and the cop escorted the manager to safety.

Giving a nod, Reed pushed open the door and the team of officers and deputies swarmed into the apartment.

It only took seconds to determine Ingersoll wasn't in the one-bedroom apartment. In fact, nothing much *was* in the apartment. A folding card table and single chair stood in the vacant living room. Empty pizza boxes were stacked on the kitchen counter. Ingersoll had lived here for two years, and yet looking at his living room and kitchen, one would guess he had moved in this morning.

Officer Drummond's fresh face emerged from

the single bedroom. "Detective? You got to see this." The young cop's voice trembled.

He'd definitely found something.

Reed stepped into the bedroom. Photos covered nearly every inch like wallpaper. Photos of Diana sleeping. Diana undressing. Diana making love. Reed's head was cropped from that one, a photo of Ingersoll pasted in its place. Other photos had been doctored, too. Hand-drawn ropes bound Diana's wrists, ankles and neck.

Rage pressed at the inside of his skull, making his head throb. "How in the hell did he get these?"

"Here." A county sheriff's detective named Mylinski waved him over. He pointed to a spot high in the corner of the room. A stool perched underneath. "Step up and take a look."

Reed stepped onto the stool. Just under eye level for him, a smooth hole had been drilled through the drywall. He lowered his eye to the hole and peered through.

Diana's bedroom spread out before him. The white flowered comforter across her bed. The chest of drawers where she kept her lingerie. The mirrored closet door that would reflect her image from wherever she stood in the room.

The lieutenant had been right not to let Reed take Ingersoll down. The skinny bastard didn't deserve to be arrested, he deserved to be killed.

"You okay?" Mylinski studied Reed through shrewd eyes, the slanting rays of the afternoon sun glinting off his bald spot.

Reed nodded, but he could tell the county detective wasn't buying it.

"Good." The detective stepped from the room.

Reed knew he'd left to give him a few minutes to compose himself. A few minutes to suck it up and get ready to do his job. The problem was, it would take him more than a few minutes to cool the anger flaming inside him, to defuse the pressure building in his head until he was ready to erupt.

He closed his eyes. He supposed he should be grateful Diana wasn't here. He never wanted her to see this. He never wanted her to know just what Ingersoll had in mind for her.

Unfortunately, he knew damn well these pictures would come out in Ingersoll's trial. It would all be exposed. To Diana. And to the world.

A footfall sounded behind him.

Reed turned around just in time to see the lieutenant step into the room.

The lieutenant usually didn't get personally involved in executing search warrants. But apparently on this case, he'd made an exception. He studied Ingersoll's montage. The overhead light reflected off his glasses, hiding his eyes, but the grim set of his mouth corroborated the sick feeling twisting Reed's gut.

"Any word?" Reed held his breath.

"He didn't show up at his ten o'clock delivery. No one has seen him since he made his first delivery this morning." The lieutenant tilted his head to the side, his stance vaguely apologetic. "Have you heard where he made that first delivery?"

Reed's gut tensed. "I'm out of the loop now, remember?"

"Not anymore." The lieutenant scuffed his shoes on the floor. "This morning, Louis Ingersoll delivered a load of fresh produce to Banesbridge prison. It's part of his regular route."

So Reed had been right. He'd been right all along. The Copycat Killer was taking his orders from Kane. Reed should feel vindicated. Instead, he couldn't muster anything but worry. "Is Diana still at the district office?"

"She was when I left."

He let out a breath he didn't know he was holding.

"All we have to do is find Ingersoll. Bring him down. And this will be over."

Reed did his best to nod. Louis Ingersoll didn't stand a chance, not with all the law-enforcement agencies in southern Wisconsin scouring the area for him. But somehow that didn't make Reed feel better. That didn't make him feel better at all.

Rubber screeched against pavement outside.

Reed dashed to the window.

A panel van swerved around the corner and roared up the street. Police cars raced behind, lights flashing, sirens shrieking.

Ingersoll.

The lieutenant dashed to the window, almost running into Reed. "What's going on?"

Reed raced for the door. "Ingersoll didn't disappear. He was just on his way home."

He took the stairs two at a time, pulling his pistol from his shoulder holster as he ran. Reaching the bottom of the stairs, he raced outside and bulled past reporters.

The air shuddered with a screech and the smack of steel on steel.

Reed pushed his legs to move faster. He vaulted a row of bushes and raced into the street.

He could see the wreck ahead of him. The van sat at an angle, its front fender buried into the side of a parked car. Red and blue flashed over a scurry of officers. The light throbbed like a strobe in the storm-darkened sky, making their movements look jerky and unreal.

Officers surrounded the van, drawing down on the driver's door. Perreth's solid form marched toward the vehicle.

Reed reached the inner perimeter of cars just as

the bulldog detective approached the van. Breath roaring in his ears, Reed joined Nikki behind her car and leveled his gun on the panel van.

"I got him. I got him." Perreth swaggered up to the van and yanked open the door.

Movement flashed from inside. A shock of red hair, the dull glint of a rifle barrel.

Reed didn't think. He didn't feel. He just closed his finger over the trigger and squeezed. Pop. He gave with the Glock's kick, letting the movement bring his gun back into position for the next tap. Pop.

Red bloomed on Ingersoll's chest. His throat. His eyes froze and he slid unmoving to the pavement.

Reed watched him, waiting for the satisfaction to fill his chest. It never came.

Ingersoll might be dead, but this wasn't over. A woman was still out there. Bound. Frightened. Alone. A woman only Louis Ingersoll and Dryden Kane knew how to find.

DIANA HAD NEVER BEEN SO HAPPY to see anyone as she was when Reed walked through the door of the district office. She scurried across the large office floor toward him, weaving through people and desks. "Reed."

A smile lit his eyes, but didn't lift the lines etching his face. If possible, he looked more tired and pale than he had in the hospital. As if something tragic had happened. As if at this moment, life was too heavy to bear.

"What is it?"

He reached out and grasped her hand, holding her fingers tight, as if afraid she'd slip away. "Not here." He pulled her across the bustling space and into one of the offices. Shutting the door behind him, he split the bent aluminum blinds with his fingers and peered out between the slats. "I have to make this fast. There's a meeting I need to get to."

Now he was scaring her. She wanted to touch him. She wanted to fold herself in his arms and know they were both safe. She leaned a hip on the edge of the desk and hugged her arms around her middle. "What happened?"

"You were right. It was Ingersoll."

She stood up, her knees wobbling under her. "I knew it. He hid that woman's identity so I wouldn't find out where the necklace came from, didn't he?"

Reed nodded. "That's what it looks like."

"I keep thinking about the way he looked at me. The time we spent alone in my apartment going through news clippings about serial killers. Clippings about Kane." She buried her face in her hands. "How long was he involved with Kane?"

"Ingersoll has been making regular deliveries to the prison for four years. Kane works in the kitchen on a regular basis, so we're guessing they pass notes to one another by tucking them into the produce or hiding them somewhere in the walk-in cooler."

"So Kane knew about me. He sent Louis to watch me."

Reed nodded.

She closed her eyes. She felt dead inside. Numb. Kane had known who she was all along. Before she'd had her first inkling about him. Before she'd gotten the nerve to track down her biological parents, he'd been watching her. Moving the pawns into place.

She shook her head, trying to clear her mind. She had to focus. The woman was still out there. The woman with the baby. "Did you find where Louis is holding Cerise Copeland? Is she alive?"

Reed turned away from the window. He stared at the blank wall behind her like a soldier waiting to accept his court martial. "We haven't found her."

Her stomach dropped to her toes. "Did you find Louis?"

"Yes."

"Let me talk to him. He'll tell me where she is." She walked to the door, expecting Reed to lead her to the jail or interrogation room or wherever they had Louis.

Reed didn't move. "I can't do that."

She'd forgotten. He wasn't on the case anymore. A pang registered in her chest. All his work had finally paid off, and he had no say about how things went down. "Who can authorize me to talk to him? The lieutenant?"

"Diana."

Why didn't he move? Why wasn't he as urgent about this as she was?

"He's dead."

"Dead?" The word lodged in her throat. So bleak. So final.

"Louis Ingersoll is dead. I shot him."

"Dead." She'd cared about Louis once. He'd been her friend, or at least she'd thought so. But she didn't feel a thing for him now. "Did you find the baby's mother?"

He shook his head.

The obstruction in her throat expanded, making it hard to breathe. She could see the poor woman in her mind's eye. Tied in an isolated place. Alone. Probably in pain. And desperately wondering if she would ever see her baby again.

She knew what she had to do. "I need to see Kane. It's time I get down on my knees."

Reed remained rooted to his spot. He shook his head. "I called the prison. He refuses to talk if police are monitoring."

"He'll talk to me."

"Diana, did you hear what I said? He won't allow us to monitor. If you walk into that interview room, you'll have to go in totally alone."

The muscles of her inner thighs dissolved, melting like butter. She willed her knees to hold her upright. "Then that's what I'll do."

"No, you won't."

She shook her head. She didn't hear him right. She couldn't have.

"Kane isn't going to tell you where that woman is, and you know it."

He was probably right. She didn't have to try very hard to remember the amusement on Kane's face when she'd nearly begged him to tell her Nadine's location. She doubted a baby would make any difference. Not to a man incapable of sympathy. Not to Dryden Kane. "It doesn't matter. I can't not try."

He blew a breath through tight lips. "I'm not going to let you go in there alone. Not after what I saw."

"What you saw?"

The planes of his face hardened. He turned away. The muscles in his back tensed, rigid under his suit coat.

"Reed, tell me." She gripped the edge of the desk, her body shaking so hard she didn't know if she was going to be sick or fall down. "It's about me, isn't it? Something Louis planned to do to me?"

She couldn't suppress the shudder that seized her. Had Louis planned to do to her what he'd done to those other women? What Professor

Bertram had tried to do to her? Or was it something else? Something she couldn't even imagine?

Something she didn't want to.

She forced herself to breathe, to think. The important thing was finding the woman Louis had kidnapped. They had no way of knowing if she was still alive. But if they didn't find her, they could be sure she wouldn't be alive for long. "It doesn't matter what you saw. Louis is dead. He can't hurt me now."

"Kane can."

She tried to swallow. Her mouth tasted like sand. "I'm willing to take the risk."

Reed's dark gaze drilled into her. "I'm not."

She stepped around the edge of the desk, close enough to touch Reed. But though every cell in her body screamed for her to reach out for him, to get lost in his arms, to let his warmth and kisses and love take all of this away, she couldn't do it.

"Let us handle this, Diana. All the agencies are working on this. We'll find her."

A pit opened up in Diana's stomach, dark and empty and aching. Nothing had changed. Reed was still taking care of her. Still sheltering her. Still trying to fix her life.

And worst of all, deep down, she wanted to let him.

She thought back to last night, to how close she

felt to Reed after he confessed to needing her, how powerful she felt when they were making love. She longed to crawl into those memories, to feel those things again, to live them.

If only they were real.

She stepped past Reed and paused in front of the door. There was only one reality now. For that poor mother. For her baby. And only Diana could do anything to change it.

Reed stepped between her and the door. Reaching out a hand, he ran his fingers up and down her arm, as if trying to warm her. "Stay in here. I'll make this as short as I can, and then we can talk. I'll let you know everything I find out. All right?"

Heat fanned over her skin, followed by cold. She drew herself up. He had to go. He had to do his job. The job he was born to do.

And she had something to do also. She just prayed she had the courage to see it through. "Go ahead."

"And you'll be here when I'm done?"

She hated lying to him. Hated the old feelings yawning inside. Hated the despair carving out her hopes and dreams and leaving nothing but an empty carcass. She drew in a deep breath and pushed the words through her lips. "Yes. I'll be here."

Chapter Sixteen

Diana stood just inside the security screening area of the prison and checked her watch for what had to be the fiftieth time. It was late, long past visitation hours. At this time, there was probably only a skeleton staff. Still, she'd never had to wait this long to get in to see Kane. But then this time she hadn't had the police or the university paving the way.

This time she was on her own.

She glanced through the metal detector and toward the door. She half expected Reed to burst through at any moment, hell-bent on saving her. But he didn't come. The mess surrounding Louis's death and the scramble to find the governor's daughter-in-law must be keeping him busy. Too busy to notice yet that she was gone.

Her throat ached. But she couldn't go back. Being with Reed undermined everything she was trying to make of herself, everything she strived to be. She couldn't fool herself into believing things would ever be different between them. As long as Reed was around, she would need him. She would fall right back into depending on him to shelter her from the world. And never again could she afford to be that weak.

A clang reached her from down the hall, a sally port sliding closed.

She blocked all nerves, all doubt from her mind. Standing straight, she pushed her heels together and faced the door that led into the prison.

The door buzzed and swung open. Corrections Officer Seides's broad shoulders filled the doorway. "Ms. Gale? Sorry it took me so long. We had a few problems tonight."

"Problems?" She braced herself, waiting for him to say that Reed had called, that he'd told them she wasn't allowed inside.

He waved a beefy hand. "Nothing big. A few inmates feeling their oats is all."

She let out a breath, trying not to show her relief. "As long as everything turned out okay."

"Yeah, we got 'em secured. You said this was urgent?"

She nodded. She'd called on the drive to the prison to try to get emergency clearance for her visit. Usually her visits had to be set up well in advance, but she hoped prison officials would let her go through based on her previous involvement with the police investigation.

And she hoped they wouldn't have to clear it with Reed. "It's very urgent. I explained the situation when I called."

"Well, let's get you back there." He held the door open and ushered her inside with a wave of a beefy arm.

They marched down the halls and negotiated the sally ports until they reached the tiny room just outside the interview room. Officer Seides switched on the camera and left to fetch Kane.

Diana stared at the screen showing the empty chairs and small table where she would once again face Dryden Kane.

Her father.

She had to stand up to him this time, had to convince him to tell her where Louis had taken his victims. But for the life of her, she had no idea how she would do it.

Time ticked by. Twice as long as before. Finally the door from the cell blocks into the interview room opened, and Seides led Kane inside. He secured Kane to the chair that was riveted to the floor and let Diana into the room.

As she lowered herself into a facing chair, a smile snaked over Kane's thin lips. "I'm so glad we could have this time alone. Just father and daughter. No police to come between us. Our private visit. As it should have been all along." His eyes glinted like cold steel.

A shiver trickled down her spine. She averted her gaze, taking in the baggy prison jumpsuit, his clean, trimmed nails and the red nylon binders securing his hands to the chair.

"You're wondering about these?" He lifted his hands against the restraints. "They seem a little cut-rate, don't they? Makes you wonder where your tax money is going."

"Where are your handcuffs?"

"It seems there was a disturbance. I suspect my deluxe steel handcuffs are being used to fasten a couple of particularly nasty individuals while the guards get everyone under control." He pulled up against the binders a second time. "Some of these inmates are true animals."

He watched her, as if eager to see the irony of his words sink in.

She kept her expression carefully neutral. "The Copycat Killer kidnapped another woman. A woman with a two-month-old baby this time."

His smile faded. "I'm not here to talk police business, Diana. I want to talk about family. How did you like meeting your brother?"

Cordell Turner.

A mix of emotion whirled through her. The

memory of how much he resembled Kane. The anger that seemed to coil inside him, ready to spring. The overwhelming desire to connect with her brother, and the resulting disappointment.

"You liked meeting him that much, huh?"

She took a deep breath, wiping the frown from her face. It was no use trying to hide her feelings from Kane. He could read her as easily as a traffic sign. "Why didn't you tell me about him right away? Why the hints and games?"

"Games can be fun. Recreational."

Games with people's emotions. Games with people's lives. "I know Cordell isn't the Copycat Killer."

He crooked a brow. "How can you be so sure?"

"Because Louis Ingersoll is."

He didn't react. Not with the twitch of a brow. Not with the quirk of his lips. "Who is Louis Ingersoll?"

She thought of Reed's theory that the two killers had communicated by passing notes hidden in the fresh produce Louis delivered to the prison kitchen. Did Kane really not know Louis's name? It was possible. Or was he merely playing more of his games? "Louis was my next-door neighbor. I thought he was my friend."

"Was?"

"He's dead."

Kane licked his lower lip. "How did he die?"

She didn't know the details. She hadn't thought to ask. All she knew was who had shot him. "He was shot. That's all I know."

"You're not in the loop? I find that hard to believe."

"I'm not. The police don't know I'm here. They didn't want me to come."

"You mean McCaskey didn't want you to come, don't you?"

She tilted her head.

Kane's thin lips pulled back in a grin. "You're too good for him, you know."

She shook her head. "I'm not going to talk about Reed with you."

"No, you came to talk about this woman. The one with a baby. The one, I'm guessing, the police can't find because they shot this Louis Ingersoll."

"Where is she? Where would he have taken her?"

"Why do you insist on doing the police's job?"

"I'm not doing their job."

"Then why are you bothering me with these questions? We have more important things to talk about."

"More important than a woman dying?"

"A lot of women die."

They certainly had at his hands. "This one has

a baby. A baby who's going to grow up without a mother."

He looked at her with dead eyes. "And that's supposed to make my heart bleed?"

Trent Burnell had been right. Kane didn't care. He wasn't capable. "Please. For me. Will you do it for me?"

"For you?"

"Please."

"You're not on your knees. I told you the next time we met, I wanted you on your knees."

She forced her legs to function, to push her up from her chair, to circle the table, to kneel down on the floor in front of him. She bit her lower lip to hide its tremble. The hard concrete seemed to suck the warmth from her body. "Tell me where she is."

"Why? Why should I do this for you? You've been more loyal to the police than you have been to me."

"I'm not with the police now."

"A start. But it proves nothing."

"What do you want from me?"

"That's easy. I want my little girl."

"I *am* your little girl."

"No, you're not. You've changed."

"I can change back. I can be whatever you want." Desperation echoed in her voice, making her cringe.

"Can you?" His eyes glinted. "Prove it."

"What do you want?"

"I want you to call me Daddy."

The word stuck in her throat. She forced it out. "Daddy."

"That sounded more like a curse." He yanked his arm upward, straining against the nylon. "Say it the right way."

Fear crept up her throat, tasting metallic, like rusty tin. She thought of Trent's warnings, of Reed's concerns. They were right. She couldn't win. She could never be that little girl again to Kane. He could manipulate and humiliate and bring her to her knees, but she'd never make him feel the way she had as a small girl. She'd never again look to her daddy with the tender, dependent, unblemished trust of a child.

She closed her eyes, blocking Kane's face from her mind. Maybe she couldn't let Reed protect her anymore. But that didn't mean she had to open herself to Kane. That didn't mean she couldn't protect herself. "I can't give you what you want. More than that, I won't. But if you really want to win back a little of the respect I had for you once, you can tell me where that woman is."

"Respect? Oh, I'll have your respect." His voice hissed, barely above a whisper.

A chill seized her, colder than anything she'd ever known. She opened her eyes.

Kane's cruel face loomed inches from her own. He stood, free of his bindings, the light reflecting off a blade in one fist. "You *will* call me Daddy. And you'll say it with love."

Chapter Seventeen

This couldn't be happening.

Diana stared at Kane, her heart tumbling in her chest. The nylon binders that had secured his hands lay on the floor. Cut. Red as blood. She couldn't make sense of it. She couldn't make sense of any of it.

He reached a hand toward her and grabbed a fistful of hair. Pulling her face toward his, he smiled. The strong scent of mint carried on his breath. "I have some things to do, then we'll talk like a father and daughter should."

Diana looked to the camera. Where was Officer Seides? Wasn't he watching? Didn't he see?

"No one's coming for you. That guard who brought you in here? He's on a paid vacation."

Seides? Paid to turn his back? Her mind stuttered. Heat burned at the edges of her self-control. She was on her own with Kane. She really was on her own.

He released her hair. He brought the knife toward her throat.

She focused on the ice-blue gleam of his eyes, waiting for the blade's sting. Waiting for death.

He grabbed the front of her T-shirt.

A tearing sound rasped in her ears as he brought the knife down, slicing the length of the shirt in one swipe. Stepping behind her, he sliced down the back. He wrenched her arms behind her, tying one piece of fabric tight around her wrists. He secured her ankles with the other.

Pressure built in her head. Memories of being tied, being left in the dark, the hopelessness of knowing she was about to die.

No.

She wouldn't give in to it this time. She couldn't. Even if he did have a knife, death would be better than what she was sure he had planned.

Kane shoved her hard with a knee. She hit the floor on her side. Breath exploded from her lungs. She gasped, trying to breathe, desperate to breathe.

Turning away from her, he grabbed the movable chairs. He jammed one under the handle of each door. He moved to the camera with the third, raising it over his head. He brought one of the chair legs hard against the device. The lens shattered. The camera ripped from the bracket holding it and swung limp from its electrical cord.

Kane set the chair on the table. Using the immovable chair that he'd been shackled to as a stepping stool, he climbed to the tabletop and reached up to an air grate in the old ceiling.

Diana watched him, lungs aching, convulsing. Even if she could breathe, she was tied. Even if she could breathe, she couldn't get away.

Kane pried the grate free of the air vent. Climbing down from the table, he twined his fingers in Diana's hair. He lifted her to her feet.

She scrambled for balance. Her scalp seared like fire.

"I told them I wanted to be transferred to a more modern facility. They should have listened. They should have done what I asked. But this place definitely has its advantages. Let me show you some of them." He lowered a lid, giving her a wink before stepping up on the table and pulling her with him.

He positioned the chair on the tabletop directly under the open vent. He climbed onto the seat.

She wasn't going to let him take her out of here. She wasn't going to let him haul her who-knew-where. She twisted in his arms. She lowered a shoulder and plowed into him, trying to knock him off the chair, trying to get away.

His arms encircled her, as strong as wire. "You can't fight me. I'm your father. I'm your god."

She pushed a scream from her lungs and thrashed against him.

A snarl twisted his thin lips. He drew back an arm and plowed his fist into her face.

Her head snapped back. Her ears rang. Blood filled her mouth. She could feel him lifting her, stuffing her through the vent. She fought through the sensations writhing in her mind. She had to clear her head. Open her eyes. Focus.

The crack and pop of metal echoed around her. She fought to regain consciousness, tugging herself to the surface of darkness only to slip back under. He was pushing her. Dropping her.

She slammed against a hard floor. Dust filled her mouth, her lungs. She sputtered and coughed, struggling for breath.

"Not very nice, but we're alone." His voice taunted in her ear. "Just daddy and little girl. Quality time. That's the important thing."

She wanted to spit in his face, to tell him to go to hell. All she could manage was a groan.

His hand smacked against her cheek. "Time to wake up, sweetheart."

She opened her eyes, lids at half-mast.

His face hovered inches from hers. His ice-blue gaze drilled into her, through her.

Her body shook uncontrollably, trembling from

the inside out. She ground her teeth together. She couldn't give in. Not to Kane. Not to panic.

Not this time.

She forced her eyes wider and tried to see where he'd taken her.

Artificial light slanted in from a transom window high overhead. Dust stirred thick in the air, making the light look dense, solid. Through the swirl, murky shapes hulked in the darkness. Unused furniture? Construction equipment? She couldn't tell. Wherever Kane had taken her, the space hadn't been used in a long time.

"After all the stories I read to you, I think you should tell me a story this time. Wouldn't that be nice?"

"A story?"

"You keep asking me questions about this copycat, but you knew him better than anyone did, didn't you, Diana?"

Louis. Nausea swirled in her stomach and pushed at the back of her throat. She had known him best. Or she thought she had. Now just the idea of him made her want to vomit.

"The papers wrote about him, but they left out a lot. I'll bet you can tell me more."

"I can't tell you anything."

"I don't believe that. Didn't McCaskey let you

see the crime-scene photos? Didn't he give you a peek of the autopsy reports?"

"No."

"I know you saw the last one. You found her spread across your bed."

She didn't have to dig very deeply into her memories to recall the shock of discovering Nadine's mutilated body. The revulsion. The fear. "You told him to do that."

"Of course. It was for your own good. Sometimes a father has to discipline his daughter. No matter how much it hurts."

"And you wanted me to tell you about it."

His teeth glinted white through the dust. "I hoped."

She shuddered.

"How did he kill her, Diana? Tell me. Was she naked? Did he cut off her clothes with a knife? Did he bare her breasts?"

She forced herself to meet those eyes, no matter how much she wanted to look away. If not for her lacy slip of a bra, her breasts would be bare right now. She would be half-naked in front of him. Those dead eyes looking at her.

Her own father.

Humiliation clogged her throat, mixing with the dust and blood.

"Did he bare her breasts, Diana?" He looked

down at her bra, as if he'd sensed her thoughts. Her fears. A smile snaked over his lips.

The gleam in his eyes made her want to retch. She held on, forcing herself to breathe. In and out. In and out.

If she encouraged him to talk, how far would he go? Would he tell her where Louis had taken his victims? Would he tell her where to find Cerise Copeland?

She swallowed a mouthful of dust. She probably wouldn't get out of the prison alive. But if she did, she could find Cerise. She could return the woman to her baby.

At least she had to try. "Yes. He bared her breasts. He cut off her bra with a knife."

THE MOMENT REED OPENED the door and stepped into that empty office, he'd known where Diana had gone. But the sting of knowing she'd lied to him again was overwhelmed by his fear.

He'd raced to the prison, lights flashing, siren blaring. He'd called on the way, finally getting hold of Corrections Officer Seides. But although Seides had assured him everything was okay, he couldn't buy it. He had to see Diana himself.

He dashed into the prison and checked through security. This time he didn't even have a gun to lock into one of the gun safes provided for police officers. He'd already had to surrender it to ballistics until the i's could be dotted and t's crossed in the investigation of Ingersoll's death. Not that it made any difference. Either way, the risk of an inmate taking it away from him was too great. Either way, he'd have to face whatever situation he found unarmed.

When he and two guards reached the interview room, Seides stood in the doorway. He looked to Reed, desperation in his eyes. "Detective, I didn't know. I—"

Reed breezed past him. The room was empty.

Acid slammed into his gut with the force of a hard fist. He scanned the smashed camera, the chair on the tabletop. The open air vent. His throat constricted. "Where does that vent lead?"

Seides stood in the doorway, staring at Reed as if he suddenly didn't speak English.

Another guard pushed past him. "It runs through the whole wing. But half of this wing is being remodeled. It's sealed off from the rest of the building. We'll have to go through the construction entrance to access it."

Reed crossed the floor to the table. "Then go. I'll go this way. And remember, he has a hostage."

He bounded onto the table, trying not to think of what Kane might be doing to her, how frightened she must be. Using the chair as a step stool, he hoisted himself into the vent. The space was cramped and dark. The metal creaked under his weight. He slid along his belly, his pulse thumping so hard in his ears, he was sure Kane could hear it echoing through the ductwork.

He crawled until the air duct split into a T. Holding his breath, he listened for something, anything that would tell him which direction Kane had gone.

A male voice rumbled through the vent.

Reed turned in the direction of the sound.

The voice grew louder, one moment threatening, the next hushed.

A faint light glowed ahead. A spot where the vent opened into another room.

Reed slid slower. He couldn't let Kane hear him. He couldn't let the killer know he'd found them. Reaching the vent, he peered down through the open hole and into a murky room.

Diana lay on the floor below in her bra and jeans, her exposed skin white against dark gray concrete. Fabric the same light blue of her T-shirt bound her ankles and wrists.

Kane stretched her tied arms over her head, looping the fabric imprisoning her arms through the slats of a wood palette piled with floor tile.

Reed gripped the sharp edge of the vent. The metal bit into his fingers, but he didn't care. He didn't care about anything but getting his hands on

Kane and pounding the bastard's head into the ground until he was dead.

As Kane focused on tying the fabric, Diana looked up. Her eyes met Reed's.

Love swept through him, hot and powerful. He nodded to her, trying to reassure her, trying to let her know everything would be okay.

That he would make it okay.

Her gaze sharpened. She stared at him, not with relief, but with anger. As if she was warning him away. As if she *wanted* Kane with her, *wanted* what he was doing to her. As if *Reed* was the problem.

What in the hell?

Kane stepped back to Diana's side. He crouched over her, shoving his face close to hers. "That's better now, isn't it?"

Reed's head pounded. What was going on? Why had Diana looked at him like that? She couldn't hate him for trying to save her. That would be stupid. More than stupid. If he didn't save her from Kane, she'd die.

"Tell me more, sweetheart. I want to know more."

"I don't know anything else."

"Yes, you do." Kane's voice exploded, sharp and angry.

Reed tensed. Kane wasn't yet under him. If he jumped, he'd land to the side of the killer. Kane could still use that knife on Diana. He could kill her before Reed had time to take him out.

He had to wait until Kane moved under the vent.

"Did he let her loose in a forest, Diana? Somewhere she could scream and scream and never be heard by anyone but him?" His eyes focused past Diana, as if reliving his own sick hunts, hearing the panicked screams, soaking in his victim's fear. His eyes sparkled with excitement, visible even through the murky dust.

Reed's ears pounded. He had to jump. He couldn't take the chance that Kane's frustration with Diana would grow. He couldn't risk the son of a bitch cutting her just because she couldn't answer his damn questions.

Kane's gaze snapped back to Diana's face. He traced the knife blade along the line of her collarbone. "Did he hunt her naked in the forest?"

"I don't know. How can I tell you where he hunted her if I don't know?"

Kane trailed the knife down over the curve of each breast, the side of the blade rasping over lace. "I know where."

"Then you tell me."

Reed's gut seized. He knew what she was doing. He knew why she'd looked at him the way she had, why she'd warned him off.

Damn.

She wanted to save the governor's daughter-in-law.

He gripped the vent's edge harder, letting the steel cut him, feeling the blood hot and sticky on his skin. All he'd ever wanted was to keep Diana safe. All he'd ever wanted was for her to be happy, for both of them to be happy.

He stared down at her, running his gaze over her golden hair, her high cheekbones, her soft, soft face. He loved her with all his heart, all his soul, all himself.

The question was did he have the guts to trust her?

Chapter Eighteen

Diana held her breath, waiting for Kane's knife to slice into her flesh, waiting for Reed to jump down from above, waiting for all hell to break loose.

Nothing happened.

She scooped in a breath, dust tickling deep in her throat. "*You* tell *me* what it was like. Unless you didn't decide that part. Unless you really don't know."

"In time." He moved the blade up to the hollow between her collarbones. "You remind me of old times. All the things I wrote to the copycat. All the things I told him to do. I need you to tell me if he did them the way he was supposed to. If he did everything right."

"I'll try."

"Good." He licked his lips. "After he hunted her, after he wounded her with the rifle, did he drag her by the hair? Did he tie her down?"

Just the things Kane had done to her.

She shuddered involuntarily. "Yes."

"Did he run a blade between her breasts?" He traced the path down Diana's body with the flat side of his blade. "Did he cut down the middle of her belly? Did he slice her all the way down?"

White noise rang in her ears, drowning out the sound of Kane's blade rasping against the denim of her jeans. "Stop. Please."

"Did he, sweetheart?"

She tried to answer. She tried to breathe. "Yes."

"Are you afraid I'll do that to you?"

"Yes." Her mind roared. She had to push away the panic. She had to hold on. She had to get him to tell her where Louis had hunted. Before Reed jumped him.

Before Kane decided to make the cutting real.

He smiled, lips pulling back from straight, white teeth. "Even from prison, I did whatever I wanted. Even from prison, I called the shots."

She had to steer Kane back to the hunt, back to the place he'd told Louis to take his victims. "Please. Don't hunt me. Just kill me now."

"You like the hunting, huh? Of course. The professor and his lame attempt to be like me. Do you still relive those moments in your nightmares, Diana?"

"Yes."

"The professor knew nothing. He was an

amateur. A phony. I can show you the real thing. I know the perfect place for a midnight hunt."

She let out the whimper pressing in her throat.

His smile grew wider. "There are islands in Lake Superior where no one lives."

The mint of his breath wafted against her face, turning her stomach. She swallowed hard. She had to hold on. She had to know.

He circled her, moving in closer over her, the knife's blade glinting in one fist. "The Apostle Islands. I'd like to take you there, Diana. Just Daddy and his favorite little girl."

He slipped the knife between the cups of her bra and pulled the sharp edge upward. The sharp steel sliced through the lace. "It's a long drive and a boat ride to the island where even the lighthouse stands vacant, but the moon glows bright off naked skin. And when the hunt is on, no one ever hears the screams."

Suddenly Kane lurched forward. The knife fell from his hand, skittering across the floor.

Reed straddled his back. Gripping the back of Kane's head, he slammed his face against the concrete with a hard blow.

Crashes as loud as thunder shook the room. Wood splintered and broke. Footsteps rained around her head.

Suddenly Reed was untying her, holding her,

wrapping his suit coat around her shoulders. "Diana. Thank God."

She pressed her face into his shoulder. Tears stung her eyes, tears she'd refused to shed until now. "The Apostle Islands. Did you hear?"

"The island with the vacant lighthouse will be swarming with local sheriff's deputies within the hour. We'll find her." He pulled her to her feet beside him. Arms still around her, he ushered her through the door the guards had rammed open and circled to the other side of a hulking piece of construction equipment. Away from Kane. Away from the voices of guards. Alone.

He gripped her shoulders. Holding her at arm's length, he searched her eyes. "He could have killed you, Diana. My God, he could have killed you." His tone was hard, balancing on the sharp edge of anger and fear.

She didn't have to hear his words to know intimately how close she'd come to death. She was still shaking with it. But she'd done what she had to, made the choices she'd had to make.

What she couldn't figure out was why he'd made the choices he had. "You didn't jump him. You waited. Why?"

The hard line of his jaw softened. He raised a hand to her face, tracing her cheekbone with one finger. "You seemed to have things under control."

Tears stung her eyes, turning Reed into a blur of color. "How did you know? Even I didn't know that for sure."

"I didn't know either. Not for sure." He brushed a strand of hair back from her cheek. "But that's what having faith in someone is about, isn't it?"

Her throat ached. Warmth radiated from the center of her chest. She'd waited a long time for him to have faith in her. But she'd waited even longer to have faith in herself.

"You don't have to worry about needing me, Diana. You don't. You can deal with life just fine on your own."

Yes, she could. For the first time in her life, she truly felt she could make it on her own. "I might not need you anymore, Reed, not like I used to. But I want you. I want to be with you. I want to share my life with you. You make me happy. And I want to be happy."

A smile touched his lips. A smile that bubbled through her blood and made her want to dance.

"I love you, Diana. I always have." He brought his lips to hers, his kiss full of need and want and love. And when the kiss ended, she looked into his eyes and found the core of strength she'd dreamed of. And she knew deep in her heart no one could take it away.

"I love you, too, Reed. And I always will."

Epilogue

Cord Turner stood in the shadow of the park shelter and watched the wedding party assembled on the north shore of Lake Mendota.

A month had passed since he'd met his sister, since he'd read in the newspaper about how she and that cop had brought down the Copycat Killer and saved the governor's daughter-in-law. A month since he'd learned about his father.

Kane was scheduled to be transferred back to the Supermax, or whatever the hell they called the place now. Fine with Cord. He didn't want to think about the bastard. He sure as hell didn't want to know him.

On the beach, the couple exchanged rings. Wind caught the bride's veil, the white cloud streaming out behind her, making her look more ethereal than an angel. Her groom held her hand, the smile on his face inspiring an empty ache in Cord's chest.

It had been years since he'd held a woman's soft

hand. Years since he'd felt the kind of joy that produced that kind of damn fool grin. He wasn't interested in women. Not even when he'd first been paroled. What was the point? None of them were Melanie. And any other woman just made the ache inside him burrow in deeper.

He turned away from his sisters, the bride with her groom, the other twin clutching hands with a man obviously crazy for her, too. He'd never know them. He could only watch them from afar. Just as he watched Melanie in the mornings when she walked from the parking ramp to her office building. He could only watch and remember. Remember all he'd thrown away.

Some people said violence ran in the blood, passed through genes from one generation to the next. Maybe it was true. He wasn't smart enough to know. His sisters hadn't inherited it. Maybe it was only passed on from father to son. And if that was the case, the violence in his family would come to an end with him.

The son of Dryden Kane.

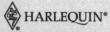

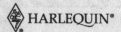

#933 BRIDAL OP by Dana Marton
Miami Confidential

Weddings Your Way agents Isabelle Rush and Rafe Montoya are sent to exotic Ladera to save a kidnapping victim, but when politicians and hired guns converge on the hot spot, passion won't be the only thing that erupts.

#934 THE HIDDEN HEIR by Debra Webb
Colby Agency

Ashley Orrick has gone to extraordinary lengths to keep anyone from finding her and her son. But when Colby agent Keith Devers catches up with her, can she trust him to believe her story when no one else will?

#935 BEAUTIFUL BEAST by Dani Sinclair

When an explosion ended Gabriel Lowe's military career and left him scarred, his life became a shadow of what it once was. But the beautiful Cassiopia Richards is determined to warm this beast's heart before an old enemy cuts short both their futures.

#936 UNDENIABLE PROOF by B.J. Daniels
Cape Diablo

Witness to a murder, Willa St. Clair seeks safety on a secluded island in the Gulf of Mexico. But when a group of killers picks up on her trail, undercover cop Landry Jones arrives to protect her, if the evils of Cape Diablo don't get them all first.

#937 VOW TO PROTECT by Ann Voss Peterson
Wedding Mission

Cord Turner never knew his father was serial killer Dryden Kane. He never knew he had twin sisters, or that former love Melanie Frist was pregnant with his son. So when Kane escapes police custody, Cord's sure going to have one heck of a family reunion.

#938 DAKOTA MELTDOWN by Elle James

When hometown girl Brenna Jensen is called in to investigate a potential killer, she's forced to collaborate with hardheaded FBI agent Nick Tarver. But as the winter ice thaws around Riverton, dead bodies surface, and the two of them are going to have to get along quickly if they're to survive the oncoming deluge.